THE SCARECROW LIVES AT NIGHT

by
Lennon Joseph

Copyright © 2022 by Lennon Joseph

All rights reserved. No part of this publication may be reproduced, stored or transmitted in any form or by any means, electronic, mechanical, photocopying, recording, scanning, or otherwise without written permission from the publisher. It is illegal to copy this book, post it to a website, or distribute it by any other means without permission.

This novel is entirely a work of fiction. The names, characters and incidents portrayed in it are the work of the author's imagination. Any resemblance to actual persons, living or dead, events or localities is entirely coincidental.

Lennon Joseph asserts the moral right to be identified as the author of this work.

Lennon Joseph has no responsibility for the persistence or accuracy of URLs for external or third-party Internet Websites referred to in this publication and does not guarantee that any content on such Websites is, or will remain, accurate or appropriate.

If you enjoy The Scarecrow Lives at Night or any other books in the series, please leave a review so others can hear what you thought. Perhaps more importantly, I would love to hear if you liked the book, and what you liked? Thank you.

Contents

Chapter 1: The Nightmare Returns 1

Chapter 2: The Haunted Farm 7

Chapter 3: The Clues 13

Chapter 4: Jacob's Secret 18

Chapter 5: Kidnapped 24

Chapter 6: Danger in the Woods 29

Chapter 7: Half Penny's Plan 34

Chapter 8: Weird Stuff 38

Chapter 9: The Fake Journal 43

Chapter 10: More Scares 49

Chapter 11: The Scarecrows 57

Chapter 12: The Necklace 64

Chapter 13: Terror on the Farm 69

Chapter 14: A Deadly Discovery 77

Chapter 1

THE NIGHTMARE RETURNS

June 2nd, 2022 was a dark and rainy night for Dark Woods. The gang – in case you have not met them yet, Tom, Eliot, Jacob, Lucy, Amelia, Sera and Jack – were now enjoying their summer and were right now playing in the arcade. The game was "Nightmares of Night Club". The friends soon realised that no matter how well they played, they simply could not get a score as high as Jack's. Jacob tried to beat Jack and win the game by using his powers.

"No, that's cheating, Jacob! That gives you an unfair advantage," Tom protested.

"That's true," Lucy agreed.

"But Jack keeps winning. Is that fair?" Jacob challenged.

"But Jack has no special powers like you and Amelia," Eliot pointed out.

"Amelia has," Jacob said.

Amelia said nothing, but the score was somehow getting higher by the second. The group were wondering why it was getting higher and higher, and then they saw that Amelia was using her powers to change the score up to 5 million points.

But then, the others in the group noticed that Jack and Jacob looked spooked. At that very moment, Jack and Jacob were experiencing a vision in which Half Penny appeared again. They had not seen Half Penny since last year during Halloween when he had kidnapped Jack. He looked a bit like a puppet, but had a terrifying face and eyes that seemed to look right through you. The whole puppet-monster fusion made him even more terrifying. There was a green lightning storm behind him, almost as if someone else was looking at him.

Half Penny then spoke: "Hello, my friends. I've got a little surprise for you. This summer, you're going to have the summer of your nightmares; you have no idea what's coming for you." Then the vision ended, and Jacob and Jack realised that they were outside, so they went back inside the arcade. The others were wondering if they were okay and there was concern in their eyes.

"Are you okay? You two just got up and walked out, and you looked like you were in a trance or something!" Eliot said.

"Yes, we are okay," Jack and Jacob said so that their friends would not be alarmed by what Half Penny told them.

The next morning, Jacob was at his house in the forest of Dark Woods alone, trying to hide the last of his journals, Journal #1. After Half Penny had told him that everyone and everything was going to die last year, he had decided to protect his journal at all cost and warn the others about what had happened.

Meanwhile, back at the building where the gate was and where Half Penny was defeated, a book that remained unaccounted for opened and unleashed one of Jacob's most terrifying monsters: the scarecrows. They appeared like skeletons dressed like scarecrows, and they walked in a mechanical, robotic style. Just looking at them would have terrified anyone. They escaped and crawled out of the book, walking away to an unknown place of origin.

But back in the woods, as Jacob was walking, he sensed he wasn't alone. Then he heard footsteps close to him and he stood his ground with his eyes and hands glowing in his flame.

Just then, something knocked him to the ground, blinding him with a bright light. It was Half Penny.

"Hello, old friend. In case you don't know, you and your friends are doomed because we're back!"

Half Penny's claw-like hand reached out towards Jacob's neck, but just then, Jacob teleported to the treehouse and called Jack and Amelia to come for a meeting to warn them about what was coming.

As the group gathered together, Jacob explained to them that Half Penny was back and had threatened to destroy them all.

Jacob sighed. "I drew those books as a way of fun because I love drawing, but now, I feel responsible for what these monsters can do. I'm sorry I got you all into this, but if we work together, we can save ourselves, the city, and many other people who may fall into the hands of Half Penny and his kind. Guys, at first, I didn't want to believe it, but when I was walking with Jack at the arcade and we saw Half Penny and he told us we have no idea what's coming for us, and then today he said we are doomed, I sensed that something was wrong. I think that when we destroyed the gate on Halloween and when we hid the books and journals, there may have been one book that was still in his possession and he is using just one book to unleash at least one monster to find out where the other two journals are and to find the other books that are hidden all over the world! And that means that anyone in possession of one of my books out there could be in grave danger."

Amelia gasped. "You mean Half Penny is back?"

Jack said thoughtfully, "So we need to find out where Half Penny's monster is going. Maybe we should go back to the place where we defeated him, 'cause maybe there's a clue or something about which monster was freed and where it's going next."

Eliot nodded. "Yeah, maybe. Let's go."

So the group got on their bikes and cycled to the Dark Woods City Hall, which had been abandoned ever since last year. But when they got there, they saw that the place was as dark and scary as the Mirror Dimension. So Jacob used his dark magic fire for some light while the others turned on their torches. But when they got to the room from where the gate was opened, they found a book titled *The Scarecrow Lives at Night*. This spelt trouble because that was one of Jacobs's most dangerous books of all! So, they decided that they had to find the chief scarecrow at all costs because if it found the other two journals, all would be lost.

Then Jacob got Journal #1 out of his jacket pocket and read from the scarecrows page in the journal.

"The scarecrow, also numbered as creature #11, is a demonic scarecrow that haunts only at the west side of Dark Woods, and only begins to haunt at sundown, and it says do not awaken at all cost!"

Inside the room from which the gate was opened, Tom and Lucy were investigating when they heard a bang. They were already terrified to be back there again after what had happened last year. Lucy clutched at Tom, her hands shaking. But there seemed to be nothing terrifying.

Just then, Lucy found a photo of Jacob and someone else standing next to him in front of the same house from where they found the "Horror Halloween" book the previous year.

Now, Tom and Lucy stared at the photo, wondering who the girl was and why the photo was here in the tower. Lucy then put it in her pocket and made Tom promise to keep it a secret for now.

Just then, they were called by Jacob and the others and told them that they all needed to find the scarecrow somewhere in the west side of Dark Woods. But just as they were about to leave, they heard a noise coming from the next room.

They were afraid, but they took hold of their weapons and Amelia and Jacob got ready to use their powers in case Half Penny was there. As they walked closely through the hallway, Jacob ignited his hand on fire. Now, his hand acted as a torch, lighting the way and giving them some light in the dark building. They were however suspicious in spite of the haunting silence, thinking that perhaps they were being watched. Half Penny had a way of creeping up on you and suddenly appearing from the shadows.

Just then, there was such a loud bang that Lucy and Sera screamed.

"Thunder," Jacob whispered.

The thunder kept roaring with a gigantic grumble. The group then saw something or someone lurking in the shadows and they stopped. When Jacob blasted the stoker, they saw that it was a 14-year-old girl.

Jacob asked, "Who are you and what are you doing here?"

The girl replied, "I'm Luna and this is my hideout. I live with my family on the outskirts of Dark Woods – my parents own a farm. Why are you here?"

Jack said, "We are here to investigate what happened here last year."

Luna seemed surprised. Then she said, "Well, here's the thing. I'm here because I want to know the same thing."

So then, the group were wondering why Luna wanted to know the same thing as they did and how she could know about what had happened on Halloween last year or why she would come here.

But just then, Jacob saw that she had a necklace that looked very familiar to him and he then asked Luna, "Where did you get that?"

And she replied, "This necklace has been in my family for 700 years."

The group looked at each other and became suspicious about how Jacob recognised that necklace around Luna's neck.

"I can tell you about the necklace," Jacob said. He explained that he saw that necklace in a dream he had about four years ago.

But just then, the group heard a noise outside of the building and went to investigate. Luna decided to follow them, very curious about how Jacob could possibly know about her necklace.

When they were outside, they realised that the noise was coming from every direction, and so they decided to ignore the noise and go to the west side of Dark Woods, since that was what it said in the journal.

As they were walking away, Luna said that the reason that she had gone there was because she saw a creature that looked like a demon outside of her family's farm in the woods.

She said to the group, "I've been trying to investigate the supernatural attack that occurred last Halloween night. I've always been curious, but when the supernatural Halloween attack happened, it opened my eyes and triggered something in me. There is something beyond the known universe out there, and I have wanted to figure it out for a long time. So that is why I came here – to find out the reason for the attack, who did it and why."

Chapter 2
THE HAUNTED FARM

The group decided to let Luna help them, and they told her about Half Penny and everything else that had happened, including Jacob and Amelia having real powers. They asked her to keep it a secret from everyone she knew, including her family, because in Dark Woods, you could trust no one! Luna and Jacob then shook hands and she said was ready to work with this mystery-solving team.

"Does your group have a name?" she asked.

"We have never thought about naming it," Eliot said.

"What if the scarecrow is on your farm on the west side of the city, Luna?" Jacob asked. "You said your farm is on the west side of the city just outside the city. The creepers and crawlers and other monsters seem to love the areas just outside the city, you know. Maybe Half Penny knows that you are investigating too and has sent one or two. You are safer with us than trying to chase deadly monsters all alone."

The farm was on the west side of Dark Woods, so Luna called her mum and asked her if it was okay for her friends to go over for the weekend and her mum agreed.

Jacob said, "Okay guys, here is the plan. Jack, Luna, Lucy and I will go to the farm and try and stop the scarecrow while the rest of you stay at the treehouse and see if anything else happens while we are gone. You need to be on the lookout just in case the scarecrow finds the journals, or worse, the books. We can't take that chance."

Jacob, Jack, Lucy, and Luna walked to the farm to investigate the scarecrow that Luna had seen days before.

Meanwhile, back in the Mirror Dimension, Half Penny was watching them from his dimension, and he now knew that the group were trying to get the scarecrows, and he was going to set a trap for them at sunset.

When Jacob arrived at the farm along with Lucy, Luna, and Jack, they walked closer and closer to Luna's family house, and her mum looked very excited to have them over for the weekend.

"Hi, come in. Luna's father is away until Monday but I have been looking forward to having you here," Luna's mother said with her arms stretched out.

She was an amazing woman. She was always happy and loved hosting people, whether it was for lunch, dinner, birthdays, you name it. She was always ready to do it and always had fun doing it.

She had prepared some mac and cheese and bread for them. For dessert, she had prepared them her famous sweet potato pie, but they were first going to go to Luna's room to wait as Luna's mother set the table.

While in there, they planned and strategised on how to capture the scarecrows and get them back into the book. They were so engaged in their planning that they didn't realise it was close to sunset. Luna's mother was the one who brought them back to reality when she knocked on the door. They were getting ready to finalise on how to send it back into its book when Luna's mom asked them to go downstairs for dinner. They were shocked that it was almost sunset.

"Kids, dinner is ready. Could you all please come downstairs?" she called as she knocked on the door.

They could hardly wait to tuck in as they sat down at the dinner table. The food smelled so good. They washed their hands and sat down, all the while thanking Luna's mother for agreeing to let them stay over for the weekend.

As they were having their dinner, there was minimal chit-chat as they did not want her to know what they were up to. They also did not want her to panic. They were going to wait until after dinner, and once she was off to bed, they would help do the dishes and then go into the cornfield to look for the scarecrows that Luna had seen earlier.

"There is plenty of food, so eat as much as you can. Do not be afraid to go for a second or even third helping," Luna's mother said to them with a smile on her face.

They all laughed at her statement and continued eating. She did not stay too long at the table. She claimed she was very tired and had to go to bed early. As soon as she left the table, they started conversing and discussing what they would do about the scarecrows that night.

Jacob said, "Guys, we need to do something because at sunset, the scarecrows come to life and it will be sunset in a few minutes, so we need to hurry up and do something."

Luna agreed. "Yes, we have to do something about this, because if those scarecrows come to life, they could hurt my family and I am not willing to risk their lives."

Jacob said, "You know very well that we wouldn't want to put…"

They heard a bark outside before he could even finish his statement, so Jacob told them to stay put. He was going to find out what the noise was about on his own.

With that, he left the house to try and figure out what the strange, mysterious sound was. He used his powers to figure out the peculiar and weird noise and sensed that it was coming from the barn. Jacob used his power of flight to investigate the strangeness around him.

He yelled as he heard Half Penny's voice and was shocked. It sent a chill down his spine. The group did not understand what was going on, so they asked Jacob what was wrong. Somehow, none of them saw Half Penny. Only Jacob and Luna did.

Half Penny cackled and said, "Hello Jacob. I see you've made a new friend and she's very familiar, I'll tell you that. Here is a hint of what's to come. You are one of the three protectors of your journals and one of them is a friend, and when the dark eclipse appears in three years' time, he will be revealed."

Luna gasped in fear and horror. "What the hell was that, Jacob?" she asked in a shaky voice.

Jacob answered, "Well, Luna, that was the eerie puppet that we've been chasing back in the city tower. Well, he wasn't always my enemy, Luna. I used to think he was my best friend. Years ago, all my life, I had been abused by others and I wanted to write stories to abuse people even worse than they abused me. But then one day, the scary creatures in my stories became very real and eventually, I was able to trap them in the books I wrote them in. I discovered that the books lead to a place called the Mirror Dimension, and last year, when it was Halloween night, when you said you saw a weird portal or light in the sky, that was a portal to it and here we are."

The rest of the team stood there fixated on the ground, wondering what was going on. Something had happened, but weirdly, only Luna and Jacob had seen whatever had happened.

"What is going on?" Lucy asked.

"Guys, please tell us what is going on. You are scaring us," Jack added.

"We just heard Half Penny," Jacob answered.

"How is it possible for you two to hear him and for us not to?" Lucy asked.

"I don't know, okay?!" Jacob answered. "We need to go into the cornfield right now if we hope to have the slightest chance of catching the scarecrows," Jacob added.

"You are right," agreed Luna.

They all walked towards the cornfield later that night and saw the scarecrows. They looked terrifying and also looked exactly like they did in the journal. Luckily, Jacob had brought both the scarecrows book and Journal#1. He had run back upstairs to get the book before they started their journey towards the cornfield.

In the cornfield, it was pitch black. The corn would scratch their hands and faces, but they could not turn back. They had to catch the scarecrows.

A few steps into the cornfield, the group heard something coming from somewhere in the cornfield and then saw a silhouette of someone rushing past them.

"Did you see that?" Jack asked.

At that moment, it rushed past them again to the opposite side.

"Yes, I did," said Luna.

"Run! Get out of here!" shouted Jacob. They did not wait to be told a second time to run.

They made a 180 turn and ran as fast as they could. Unfortunately, Jack tripped and fell. Something started dragging him into the cornfield, and all he could do was scream in fear and terror as he disappeared into the centre of the cornfield. They had not even noticed that he had fallen until he started screaming. They had to go back and save him. They could not leave him behind. They all ran to try and save him but whatever was pulling him was so fast and strong.

"Jacob, reach for my hand!" Lucy shouted as she stretched her hand towards him.

"I am trying, but this thing is too strong for me!" Jacob shouted back. It continued dragging him on the ground, and he had to struggle to hold his head up high so as not to get his face scratched.

When the group made it to the centre of the cornfield, Jacob turned and lay on his back, opened his hands, and threw a magic blast in the sky to try and find the scarecrow. Unfortunately, before anything could even happen, they were attacked and knocked out, and the next thing they knew, they were waking up in the house.

Everyone groaned and winced in pain. How did they get to their beds? That was all they wondered in their minds.

Luna was the first to ask, "What happened?"

Luna's mum then answered. "I don't know. I just found you in the cornfield unconscious. I heard screams while I was in my bedroom and so I decided to come and see what was going on, only to find you lying unconscious on the ground. What were you doing out there at that point in time? How did I not even hear you leave the house?"

Jacob answered, "Umm... we wanted to try some corn from the field, but we got tired and fell asleep."

She looked at them with questioning eyes as if to let them know that she was not buying that excuse, but it was the only excuse that came to his mind. They looked at each other in confusion, wondering what exactly had happened. They did not want to tell Luna's mother what had happened because that might put her in danger, and then again, they did not know whether she would believe them.

Jacob remembered seeing the scarecrow with his own eyes. Half Penny was making good on his promise to destroy them. One would have found it hard to believe that Half Penny was once Jacob's friend.

Chapter 3
THE CLUES

Since it was already morning, the group dragged themselves out of bed with their heads throbbing in pain and their bodies aching, and went downstairs and started reading Journal#1 while eating breakfast to see if there was anything in it about what the scarecrow could do or what its weaknesses were. That was what Half Penny was after, and he was willing to go to great lengths to find it. Unfortunately, the journal said that its weakness was unknown. They were in big trouble because it would be tough to trap it in the book if they didn't find out what its weakness was.

Meanwhile, back in Dark Woods, Eliot seemed to have found nothing about what happened to Dark Woods until he saw a weird symbol on his clue board, which made him think that maybe Half Penny was watching them.

Tom, Sera, and Eliot had decided to go back and try to play detective and figure out what had happened to Dark Woods, but Amelia had decided to go to sleep. They would wake her up if they needed her.

They had been searching for clues, but their search seemed to bear no fruits. They were all tired from searching, but they were not ready to leave until they found what they were looking for. Even if it was only one clue, at least that would mean that they were getting closer to figuring out what had happened. Eliot had even designed a clue board that included all the previous clues they had figured out along the way. Something was out of place, though. The clue board seemed to have been rearranged, and he had not done it. Everything seemed out of place. The clues were not in the order in which he had arranged them.

It was as if someone had rearranged them and was trying to throw them off the trail.

As he leaned closer to confirm his fears, an eye popped out of the centre of the clue board, looked directly into his eyes, and disappeared. He screamed and jumped back.

"Did you see that?" he asked.

"See what?" Sera asked.

"You didn't see that?"

"See what, Eliot?" Tom asked.

"I noticed that the clue board had been rearranged and the clues were not in the order in which they were before. Everything seemed messy and so I leaned in to try and figure out what was going on. Just as I was about to start putting them back in order, an eye popped out in the middle of the board, looked me straight in the eyes and disappeared. Are you sure you didn't see it?" Eliot explained.

"Are you sure that is what you saw?" asked Sera as if doubting him.

"Yes, I am sure of what I saw. I am not crazy. The eye looked familiar," Eliot said firmly. "I believe that eye belongs to Half Penny," he added.

"What!" shouted Sera and Tom in unison.

"Yes, that was Half Penny. He has distinctive eyes that are easily recognisable. I think he is watching us. He knows our every move. He has even seen the clue board and now knows that we are getting closer to figuring out what happened at Dark Woods."

Tom and Sera stood there fixated on the ground, unable to even say a word. They were in shock from realising that Half Penny was watching them. They felt that Jacob or Amelia could help them if they came across Half Penny, but now they were on their own.

Back at the farm, Jacob and Lucy were talking to each other when Lucy suggested that they stop getting nervous all the time and have fun for once, to which Jacob reluctantly agreed. They had been trying to figure out what had happened to them all day.

Jacob asked, "So what should we do now?"

Luna said, "I have an idea. Jack said that you have dark magic, so can you show it to me?"

Jacob sighed and said, "Fine, just follow me to the cornfield so your mum won't know about this because what she doesn't know won't hurt her."

Luna had heard of Jacob's powers but had only seen them when the scarecrow attacked them the previous night. At first, she could not believe it, but after yesterday, she was even more curious to see the kind of magic Jacob possessed.

They dashed to the cornfield, and when they arrived at the middle of it, Luna asked Jacob if he had the power of fire, to which he opened his hand and purple magic fire appeared.

Luna was astonished and found it very impressive and amusing. Jack then asked if they could go and slide down a sand mountain, and Luna and Lucy thought that that was a great idea considering it was the summer, but Jacob didn't want to do it because he had been trying to stop Half Penny for years and it was just hard to catch a break.

After a bit of persuasion from the others, Jacob gave in. Jack, Luna, Jacob, and Lucy slid down the sand hill, and as they were laughing from the sheer fun of it, Tom turned to his left and was just in time to see Jacob about to hit a giant rock.

"Look out!" he screamed, forcing the others to look towards the direction he was facing.

They saw Jacob fall on his side and roll down the hill. He had missed the rock by only a few inches. He was not entirely out of danger, though. There was another huge rock in front of him, and this time around, he was barely out of its way. They heard him screaming and rushed to help him, but he levitated himself into the air to save himself from getting crushed. He then levitated himself to the ground lower and lower. They stood there looking at him, mesmerised at what he had just done. Every day, they discovered some new magic from Jacob. Jacob himself was also in awe as he had not done that before.

"Are you okay?" they asked him while standing there in admiration.

"Yes, I'm fine," he answered, trying to dust himself off. "We had better head back home before Luna's mother comes looking for us," he added.

They all walked in silence, trying to figure out what exactly had happened and letting the fact that Jacob had very powerful magic sink in. Everyone was in awe.

"Can we cook outdoors?" Luna asked her mother.

"Oh yes! I love those outdoors barbecues!" Lucy said gleefully.

"As long as you all stay out of trouble. No trips to the cornfield in the dark, okay?"

The group sat down at the table while Lucy, who had often helped her mother with backyard barbecues before, cooked aromatic meat on the grill. She was reaching into her pocket for a hanky when the photo she had found at the City Hall fell to the ground. She looked at the picture she had found in the City Hall, and Jacob saw her do it and stared at the photo too, even though he was at the table some distance away.

He was still trying to wrap his head around everything that had happened that Halloween and what had happened while they were sliding down the sandy hill. They had never had an eventful Halloween like that one. They all tried to pretend like they were okay, but in the real sense, everyone was traumatised. No one had even dared to mention what had happened at the hill, but he knew they were a curious lot and would ask at some point. For now, he was going to let it slide and pretend like nothing had happened until one of them was courageous enough to speak up.

Lucy had the most challenging time coping and accepting what had happened to them over Halloween. She often had nightmares and would wake up screaming in the middle of the night and her clothes full of sweat. She had become withdrawn from people and had even changed from the outgoing and outspoken girl she previously was into a quiet and reserved person. She would lock herself in her room almost all day, and when she was not, she would sit outside and stare blankly into space. They had tried their best to get her back to the girl she used to be, but it was proving to be complicated.

Lately, though, she had been trying to keep herself busy, and so most of the time, you would find her cooking. She made finger-licking meals.

Lucy looked away from the picture and locked eyes with Jacob. She knew that he had been watching her. They had all been worried about her, and to be honest, she was worried about herself too, but she was not going to dwell on that at the moment.

"Hey, would you mind telling us what happened earlier today at the sandy hill?" she asked Jacob.

He knew he was cornered because she had found him staring at her. She was brilliant. She was trying to divert the attention from herself. He broke his gaze just in time to see everyone staring at him. Finally, someone had addressed the elephant in the room. Lucy had finally asked the question that everyone was dying to ask.

He looked at them one by one as if trying to read their minds. What was he going to tell them? Most of the time, he would discover a new power before even he could master the one he already had. The best part about it, though, was the fact that he knew no matter what, he would always count on them to come through for him. They had been there when he had first found out about his powers and had helped him accept the fact that he would always be different from them.

Chapter 4
JACOB'S SECRET

Lucy had decided she would ask Jacob about the photo, but then Luna's mother rejoined them and she had to wait until they were all kids alone in the backyard, enjoying the evening breeze. She took the photo out of her pocket again and held it in front of Jacob.

Jacob gasped audibly and asked in a furious tone, "I hadn't seen that clearly but I did see you with a photo! Where did you get that, Lucy?!"

As he asked this, he rushed towards Lucy to grab the photo from her hands. Lucy backed away from him in an attempt to keep him from taking it. In his rage, Jacob used his telekinetic ability to lift Lucy in the air while interrogating her about it and demanding that she give the photo back.

Luna and Jack were taken aback by how fast the situation had escalated. One minute there were all talking and the next Lucy was floating in the air like some piece of paper blown by the wind. They had never seen Jacob get so riled up by something.

"Jacob, stop... what are you doing?" begged Luna.

"Please put her down, you're hurting her!" added Jack.

As Lucy struggled, the photo fell from her hands and Luna caught it just in time. Jacob immediately released Lucy and moved towards Luna. They both stared at the picture for a while and Luna wondered who the girl next to him was. Before she could ask, Jacob snatched the photo out of Luna's hands and put it in his pocket.

"I'll take that, thank you very much!" he said with a snap.

"What is all the secrecy about? Why won't you let us see the photo?" asked Luna inquisitively.

"Listen here, guys, the contents of this photo are none of your business, and I would appreciate it if none of you ever ask me about this photo again, are we clear?" Jacob said curtly, and without waiting for a response, walked away.

The sun was high up at this time of the day. White, fluffy crowds drifted across the clear, blue sky. As Jacob walked further away, the group looked amongst them with worry. It had come as a surprise to everyone how guarded Jacob had become about the photo.

Everyone was lost in their own thoughts when an eerie scream from Jacob pierced the air. They were all startled for a split second before they all rushed to him to see what was wrong. Everyone was concerned and they all started asking questions at once.

"Oh my goodness, what happened?" Luna was the first to ask.

"Are you hurt or something, what's wrong?" added Jack, concerned.

Even Lucy, who had gotten into a confrontation with Jacob earlier, felt worried sick for him. Jacob lay still, not saying a word. He could not feel anything. Just a moment ago, he had felt a sharp pain in his head. It was as if someone had put a bullet through his skull because it hurt like nothing he had ever experienced before. His mind was a whirlwind and he was pretty sure he had blacked out for a few minutes.

When he came around, he woke up to the concerned faces of his friends. They all look so worried about him and for a second, he felt like a jerk for how he had treated them earlier, especially Lucy.

"Are you okay, Jacob? You scared us there," Jack said when Jacob woke up.

"Can you tell us what happened?" asked Lucy, who had been quiet for a while.

"I don't know myself. I was just walking when I felt a very sharp pain and I guess I blacked out after that," Jacob replied, struggling to sit up.

"Are you still in pain?" Luna asked.

"That's the strange part; I do not feel anything at all at the moment," Jacob replied.

The others looked at each other in confusion. They all thought it was strange, but no one said anything. After all, they had experienced many stranger things, especially during last year's Halloween. Besides, there was nothing normal about a 15-year-old boy with telekinetic abilities.

Just when they all thought Jacob was okay, he suddenly went into a violent spasm that rocked his whole body. His eyes suddenly went white and rolled back into his eye sockets. It was as if he was seeing a vision or something. In his mind, Jacob was taken back to the house of horrors. This was the last place he had seen the photo until it appeared in Lucy's hands. He could not understand why he was getting this vision now. An image of the red brick house also suddenly appeared in his vision and he could see Half Penny in the shadows with his malicious grin.

If you didn't know any better, you would assume he was having an epileptic episode. Everyone was visibly scared now. They were too scared to shake him back to reality so they just let the episode play out for a few more minutes until he calmed down. Jacob slowly opened his eyes. He had a distant, faraway look in his eyes.

Luna was the first to speak. "Has that ever happened to you before?" Being the newest member to join the group, Luna was more surprised than anyone else and her voice was full of concern.

Jacob was too dazed to say anything but stare at them.

"No, it hasn't happened before, at least not when we are all together," Jack answered for Jacob.

Lucy and Jack helped Jacob sit up against a stone. They were still in the cornfield, and the breeze from the cornfield provided the much-needed relief from the scorching sun. Luna could now not help but wonder if there was any correlation between these episodes Jacob was having and the photo he was trying hard to keep from them. If the episodes had never happened before, then they must have been triggered by something.

These thoughts prompted her to ask, "So how exactly did you get your powers, Jacob?" with genuine curiosity. She had been meaning to ask this question ever since she found out that Jacob and Amelia had supernatural abilities, but there was never a right time.

"I cannot really tell for sure. All I know is that for as long as I can remember, I have had these powers. Amelia too cannot tell you how she got hers," Jacob answered. "I think it's one of those things that just happen for mysterious reasons."

"Okay, but can you tell us what you saw just earlier? You looked like you were in a trance. Did you have a vision or something?" Jack asked.

"Yes, I saw the pho--" Jacob started to say he saw the photo but stopped himself just in time. Instead, he said, "I saw a vision of the red brick house outside the city of Dark Woods and a fleeting image of Half Penny in the background."

Everyone gasped.

"Is that a sign that we should go visit the place? For all we know, Half Penny could have trapped another innocent soul in that doomed house!" Lucy said shakily.

"You're right, maybe someone needs our help. But if we have to go to such dangerous grounds, we'll need the whole team, especially Amelia. Her powers can come in handy," Luna added sensibly.

Unaware of the impending doom, the group unanimously agreed to later pay a visit to the red brick house. But first, since they were all a little worn out and Amelia was not there yet, they decided to go back to Luna's house.

The savoury smell of creamy, homemade, baked macaroni and cheese welcomed them in the house. This was Luna's favourite dish and her mum had decided to treat her and her friends to her special. As if on cue, you could hear some of their stomachs grumble. Luna practically ran into the kitchen.

"Take it slow, young lady, you will fall or break something," Luna's mother chastised gently. "Now, help me set the table for you and your friends."

"Music to my ears!" a hungry Luna answered delightfully.

The two finished setting up the table and Luna invited her friends to eat. Everyone served themselves a plateful and ate silently.

"Luna, turn on the TV. I heard that the Mayor was going to make a special announcement today," Luna's mother said in an attempt to break the profound silence.

"Sure, Mother," answered Luna.

The TV turned on just in time for them to get the message: "We interrupt this program to bring you an important live briefing from the Mayor of Dark Woods about the incident of last year's Halloween."

They were immediately taken to a live press briefing by the Mayor.

"People of Dark Woods," the Mayor said, then paused and nodded solemnly, perhaps to indicate that this was a very serious matter. "I decided to call this press briefing to address what happened at Halloween in our city and to lay to rest all the rumours circulating. We all know to some degree what happened here at Halloween, and all the destruction that resulted from the fiasco. While many speculations and rumours have come out as to what was the cause of all the destruction and chaos, I want to assure you that my office will not rest until the truth comes out. We are currently looking into the cause of everything. We urge our citizens to remain calm and stop propagating rumours that could cause unrest and ruin the peace in our beautiful city. My office is working hand-in-hand with the police and we intend to get to the bottom of this matter. Houses don't just start burning by themselves, and people do not get murdered by invisible forces. One of my theories is that a gang of people created a smokescreen through fire and went on a killing rampage, using the darkness and smoke as a veil. We are trying to investigate why no one saw these people," Mayor Stanford Haydon said. "I will now respond to a few questions from members of the press."

"Is it true that supernatural forces are behind what happened here in Dark Woods?" the first reporter asked.

"Those are unfounded rumours; we do want to cause any panic to the general public. As far as the Mayor's office is concerned, we believe that someone caused the hallucinations to scare us. People should stop speculating until we release an official statement about what happened," the Mayor replied.

"Is it true that there is someone kidnapping women and kids? Do we have a serial killer in our midst?" asked the second reporter.

"There are no reports of a serial killer or mass murderer on the loose. As I said, the police, and I also, believe that some guerrilla army attacked our city during Halloween, but somehow no one saw them. If there was a serial killer, my office would not rest until they caught the culprit. But yes, we have heard strange kidnappings and wild reports from ex-victims of monsters. We believe that these victims were hallucinating as a result of a drug that the doctors have not been able to identify yet. We urge our citizens to stop propagating malicious rumours that could cause tension and unrest amongst people," Mayor Stanford replied. "I am going to end this press briefing at this point. Keep safe and report any suspicious activity to the police. Thank you and goodbye."

The kids looked amongst each other silently. They knew better about what was happening and that Half Penny was the cause of all the chaos in the town. But who would believe that Half Penny or the Mirror Dimension existed unless they experienced it themselves? And who would believe that Half Penny and his monsters were behind the massacre? They were afraid to go to the police because there were so many things they would not understand. How would they explain the powers that Jacob and Amelia had or how they had gotten them in the first place? How would they explain that there was a supernatural force – Half Penny – who was the cause of everything? How would they explain the journals or the Mirror Dimension?

Chapter 5
KIDNAPPED

There would just be a lot to unpack should they decide to go to the authorities. Not to mention, they were not sure how much blame would fall back on them. The children even found it difficult to open up to their own parents. This was a secret they would take to the grave. For now, they were going to do anything within their power to try and stop Half Penny from wreaking more havoc on their town.

Jack was not aware that at that very moment, two police officers had just arrived at his house to ask if they could ask him a few questions. When he was rescued the previous year, he had told the police all about Half Penny, but the next thing he knew, he was being tested for a drug that may have cause the "hallucinations". There was no way the police would believe Half Penny existed unless they met him face to face. They were trapped in the middle of a real nightmare, and no one could believe them.

Jack rode ahead on his bike to go and pick Amelia. The others waited for them at the entrance of the farm. The two did not take long; within a short while, they were back and they all rode to the outskirts of the city of Dark Woods.

Jacob seemed to be in more haste to get there as he rode ahead of the group.

"Jacob, wait for the rest of us. It is not a competition on who gets there first!" Amelia shouted after Jacob.

The others laughed. She was becoming talkative as she got used to being a part of the group. She had been very quiet; perhaps because she had lived alone for a long time before they found her the previous year.

"Let him be, Amelia," Luna said, "He has been in an awful mood ever since Lucy found a photo of him with some girl".

"A girl?" Amelia asked with a mischievous grin. "Did he say who the girl was?"

"That's the thing, he refuses to talk about anything to do with the photo. Did you know that he used his telekinetic ability on me when I wouldn't give him the photo? I thought he would suddenly let me crash to the ground and I was so terrified," Lucy said.

That news shocked Amelia so much that she nearly lost her balance on the bike.

"That is just unbelievable! I mean, I know Jacob can be irrational sometimes and often uses his powers for all the wrong reasons, but I never thought he would use it against any of us. That is just unacceptable. We ought to have a talk with him about this," Amelia stated. She was far knowledgeable beyond her years.

After this declaration from Amelia, they rode on in silence until they arrived at the red brick house. They found that Jacob had already parked his bike and was waiting for them. They all knew that despite his powers, he was too chicken to dare enter the house himself. Amelia chuckled to herself at the thought.

They stealthily walked inside just in case it was an ambush and Half Penny was waiting for them. The house looked deserted. There was broken glass everywhere and the putrid smell of urine was so intoxicating that it was hard to breathe freely. The window panes were broken and there were dirty wrappers of takeout foods everywhere. The state of the house was deplorable, but then again, this was expected as prisoners may have been chained in different rooms here.

"Looks like there is nobody here," announced Jack after being the first one to enter all the rooms.

"Yeah, the state of this house is not even fit for a human being, let alone an animal!" Amelia said in disgust.

"You're right. I would gladly welcome death than being held hostage in this hellhole!" Luna added with conviction.

"Well, I guess we thought wrong; Half Penny is not keeping anyone here," Tom said. "But why would he try to lure us here then? Perhaps it's just you he wanted to lure here, Jacob. Let's head back before it starts getting dark."

Even though everyone was convinced they had been wrong, Jacob could not help but feel there was a reason this house came to his vision. He could not help shake the feeling that they were there for a reason, or in some twisted way, they had been manipulated to come here.

"Where are our bikes? Oh my God, somebody took our bikes!" Amelia shouted once outside.

They all ran to see and true to her words, their bikes were all missing from the places they had parked in the backyard.

"How are we going to get back home now? It is such a long distance and I don't think I have it in me to walk all the way," Eliot moaned in frustration.

"Even If we were to walk, there is no way we will be there before sundown," Lucy added.

"Well, we can keep standing here and wasting time, or we can start walking," Jacob said testily.

"Geez, no need to get testy, we are all just exasperated by the idea of having to walk home. Let's go, guys," Tom said in a reprimanding tone.

As the group set out to walk home, suddenly, a van approached them from behind. There was a man behind the wheel and he asked if the group wanted a ride. They were all too grateful to even register "stranger danger" and they all hopped into the back of the van.

"Thank you so much, sir, we really appreciate your help," Amelia said once they were settled.

It was rather dark inside the van as the windows were tinted a dark blue.

"Well, don't thank me yet…" the man said before breaking into a familiar malicious laugh.

"Half Penny!!!" they all screamed in unison.

Soon, as this realisation hit them, they discovered that they were chained to their seats. As they all struggled to get out of their seats, the van made a U-turn and started driving into the woods. At this point, they were all screaming and struggling to free themselves from the chains.

"Jacob, do something! Throw a magic blast or something, do something… anything!" Lucy screamed hysterically.

"I can't do anything; my hands are tied to my back!" Jacob screamed back.

"What happened to your power?" Tom asked with a jeer. "You were very powerful just a few hours ago."

"Oh my God, we're going to die! He's going to kill us this time!" Luna cried out loudly.

"Everybody be quiet! I cannot concentrate on my powers if all of you keep screaming!" Amelia shouted above everyone else.

They all went quiet. Amelia let out one ear-piercing scream and with all her powers and strength, the chains that were holding her suddenly came undone. The first person she released was Jacob because he had powers and would easily help the others. Jacob, after being released, decided to first throw a magic blast towards Half Penny. The blast disoriented the driver and he lost control of the van. He drove in a zigzag motion before having a head-on collision with a tree.

By this time, Amelia had already freed the others and once the van hit the tree and came to an abrupt stop, they were all thrown forward. Luckily, nobody was hurt. Jacob blasted the doors open and they are scrambled to get out. They all expected Half Penny to be passed out on the steering wheel but when they came around to the driver's seat, nobody was there. It was as if Half Penny had magically disappeared from the scene of the crime.

"He was right here! Did he vanish?!" Luna screeched in horror.

Everyone else was spooked at this point. Jack had the eerie feeling that they were being watched.

"We need to get the hell out of this place, fast!" Jack said impatiently.

"How, genius? Did you suddenly grow wings and you're now going to fly us back home, huh?" Luna asked sarcastically. She did not intend to be mean but at this point, she was out of patience for anyone or anything.

"Guys! Guys! Look! Here are our bikes!" Amelia screeched with excitement.

"Amelia, this is not the time for jokes, please," Luna said testily.

"No, for real, our bikes are here!" Amelia answered affirmatively.

True to her words, their bikes were there in the boot of the van. Hastily, everyone took their bikes and they all speedily drove away.

"Let's see what else is in the van," Jacob suggested, and Tom and Lucy followed him into the van while the others stood outside.

Suddenly, there was a loud bang inside the van and a blinding greenish light, and then everything went silent.

"What's going on? Tom? Jacob? Lucy?" Eliot called apprehensively.

Silence.

Amelia pointed inside the van with her right hand, and a brilliant yellowish light shone inside the van. The van was empty! Jacob, Tom and Lucy had vanished!

Chapter 6

DANGER IN THE WOODS

Tom opened his eyes slowly and immediately began to choke. There seemed to be very little air in the dimly-lit room. He lifted his head, which was slumped on his chest. His neck hurt with the strain of holding his slumped neck for perhaps half an hour. The back of his head had almost cooled off now.

Tom saw the form of Jacob still lying on the floor. He was not bound, that was for sure.

"Jacob!" he called. He tried to keep his voice low, but he wanted Jacob to hear his voice. "Jacob!"

Tom realised that Lucy was gone. Had that maniac really taken her with him? He felt a pang of fear for her. This made the situation even more of an emergency. He lifted the chair a little and thudded it on the floor. Jacob still lay oblivious.

Throwing caution to the wind, Tom called loudly, "Jacob!"

Jacob slowly opened his eyes. He grimaced and groaned, his hand touching his nose and chin. He sat up with quite some difficulty.

Then his eyes seemed to focus as he saw Tom. "Tom! Where... you okay?" He felt his chin.

"Come on, Jacob! That psycho took Lucy with him, I think. He knocked us out with some form of spray. We have to get out of here. Why do you keep losing and regaining your powers? What will happen when we are in danger and need your help? You could have saved us that one time and saved Lucy."

Jacob touched his forehead and closed his eyes. "I remember. Now I remember. Lucy. We need help, Tom!"

Tom stamped his bound feet in frustration. "You were the one helping us earlier today! You are not bound; get me off this chair and let's move! Time is running out!" He instinctively looked up at the clock on the wooden wall. It was eighteen minutes past four in the morning.

Jacob got to his feet and swayed a little. "Something knocked me out, Tom." He began to undo the bonds that held Tom's hands to the chair.

"Half Penny knows you can do nothing when you are unconscious, Jacob. But couldn't you have thrown some smoke or fire at him?"

"He must have moved too fast," Jacob replied. "Do you think the others are in danger?"

Tom winced and gasped as circulation was restored to his hands and feet. It was a painful experience. He had to sit, flexing his numb legs and hands slowly for two minutes before he could get to his feet.

"Jacob, we need to be out of here now," he said. He opened the cabinet. "Saw him getting weapons here." He looked into the cabinet. "Nothing there but funny cylinders and paints."

They walked out to the passage that joined this room.

"Look at this," Jacob spoke as he faced the door.

Tom looked. There were wires tied around the inner door knob that ran into a plastic and metal contraption in a small wooden box placed on the ground. The top of the contraption had something like a stopwatch that ticked.

"It's a bomb!" Tom said promptly. "The murderous monster left a bomb here!"

"Six minutes eighteen, seventeen, sixteen seconds," Jacob read as the watch ticked.

"Six minutes before the thing goes off!" Tom exclaimed. "We'd better get out of here, now! Unless you are able to use your powers to stop the bomb."

Jacob stretched his hand towards the bomb. Instead of stopping, the timer began to move faster than before as the blue light from Jacob's hand shone on it.

"You are making it worse!" Tom yelled. "Now it's counting faster and is down to four minutes!"

"We can't open the door without moving the box or the wires," Jacob gaped. He stared at Tom in horror. "We are trapped!"

Tom looked around frantically. "Why did he leave it near the door?"

"So that anyone trying to enter or leave the house detonates the bomb," Jacob guessed brilliantly.

"Fair enough," Tom said, his mind working fast. "But how did he leave the house? There was no way he could leave the bomb here and leave by the same door."

"Now you are thinking, mate." Jacob patted Tom on the shoulder. "And we have to find that other exit in… three minutes forty-eight seconds going by the timer!"

They ran back to the living room or whatever that scantily-furnished room where they had been held was. They frantically tried the tinted windows.

"No way out," Tom said in a despairing voice. "Metal bars on the inside, close together." He shook the bars. "Too strong! There must be a way! I don't want to be here when the thing goes off!"

"There is one thing we can do," Jacob said calmly. "I can teleport us both out of here."

"You can? Then why are we wasting time?" Tom asked in disbelief. "Didn't that occur to you at first?"

"Just that I keep losing confidence in my powers and am still learning what they do. Like when I thought they would stop the bomb when they only made it tick faster."

He grabbed Tom's hand and whooooosh! They were now outside the cabin, about ten yards away.

There was a great explosion as the doors and the windows of the cabin blew, filling the air with orange flames.

"Do you think that will bring the fire department and police here?" Tom asked.

"Of course not, silly. We are in the Mirror Dimension. Did you notice that that was the Mirror Dimension version of the red brick house?"

"Oh. We must see if the real red brick house still exists," Tom said.

"It probably does," Jacob said. "We must find Lucy – and the others."

A police car skidded to a halt six feet from the rest of the group. An officer yelled from inside the van.

"What's going on here, kids?"

The two policemen walked over to where Eliot, Amelia, Sera, Luna and Jack stood.

"A monster kidnapped us and took our friends away," Luna said, and the policemen glanced at each other and then chuckled.

"You are not those kids telling weird tales about some monsters, are you?" the other officer asked sternly. "If you go about spreading rumours, you'll be punished."

"Somebody gave us a lift towards the city and then ran off," Eliot said hurriedly, nudging Luna.

"Wait. I know you, son. You are the kid who went missing last Halloween, aren't you? Are you looking for more fairy tales out here? You kids are nothing but trouble. Whose van is that?"

"The driver vanished," Jack said.

There was no point in telling these policemen that a monster named Half Penny who seemed like the most terrifying puppet had kidnapped their friends as they were investigating the van. According to the police, that was a fairy tale.

The police then radioed for a tow-truck to haul the truck back to the city. They warned the group to stay out of trouble "and stop making up tales and getting into mischief or you'll get into real trouble."

Chapter 7
HALF PENNY'S PLAN

"We need to find Lucy," Tom said to Jacob. "The others are probably worried about us, but Lucy is in the hands of that creepy monster and she is in the Mirror Dimension too."

"Let me feel," Jacob said, signalling to Tom to stay quiet.

"What do you mean 'feel'?"

Jacob closed his eyes and placed the tips of his forefingers on the sides of his head, his body very still.

"Hold my hand," Jacob said.

The next thing Tom knew, he and Jacob were flying through the misty woods of the Mirror Dimension with its rather dour and greyish colours. Now they were standing near a ruin that seemed about to crumble – the walls were burnt a black colour and the entire roof had fallen in. But a passage led into the darkness inside the ruin. Tom thought he knew a ruin that looked exact like that in the city. In fact, this seemed like their own house back home – but in ruins!

They hesitated as they came to where the darkness began, leading into the passage under the fallen roof.

Then they heard a voice roar, "So you dare to come here!"

Tom felt a shiver run up his spine, but Jacob yelled, "We want the girl you kidnapped."

There was a loud whooshing sound and then a gale of wind seemed to blow both Jacob and Tom down the passage unceremoniously, knocking them against the floor and the wall. Now they were in what would have been Lucy's room inside Tom, Eliot and Lucy's home back in the real world.

Half Penny seemed even more terrifying in the light of a lamp that seemed to be burning in a red, fiery flame. Tom had never seen a blood-red flame before. He stared, fascinated.

Then they heard a sound and saw Lucy bound and gagged on the bed.

"Good thing you are here," Half Penny growled. "I'm showing you what will happen to your home in the near future. And to every remaining house in your cursed city!" And he gave his terrifying laugh.

And now, Tom and Lucy got to see Half Penny and Jacob locked in a battle of power. Jacob threw a ball of flame towards Half Penny, but Half Penny reached out and sent it back like a boomerang. It came back as ice-cold water and drenched Tom and Jacob, making them shiver. Jacob pointed his hands at Half Penny and orange fire flew from his eyes and hands.

Half Penny took a step back and staggered, but he managed to put out the fire instantly and the room was filled with smoke that made them all choke. Jacob then grabbed Lucy and Tom's hands and teleported them back to where the van had been when the three of them vanished. The van was gone – so were the others. They did not know that the police had taken away the van.

So Jacob did his magic again and now they were walking behind the others, who were pushing all the bikes towards the city.

"Hey, wait for us!" called Jacob, and the others turned in surprise.

Tom, Jacob and Lucy told the others what had happened.

"You should have seen how our house looks like in Half Penny's plan in the Mirror Dimension," Tom said, shaking his head. "Total ruins."

"We won't allow that to happen," Jacob said.

"Then we need to find the journal and stop the scarecrow or scarecrows," Luna said.

"Hold my hands, all of you," Jacob said, and they did.

The next thing they knew, they were teleported back to Luna's backyard.

"Scarecrows love farms," Jacob said. "The answer to stopping the scarecrow is right here on Luna's farm. Since we know that Half Penny has a dangerous plan to turn the entire city into ruins and intends to use the scarecrows in the next part of his plan in finding the journal, we should sabotage his plan by stopping the scarecrow in the cornfield."

"It will be night soon and this is our last night here before we all go back to our homes tomorrow," Eliot said. "So if we are going to try to stop them, this is the time do it."

"I'm scared," Sera said.

"A scarecrow's job is to scare anyone that sees it, so don't let them know," Jacob said to her. "We only have one problem. There are many scarecrows in the cornfield and we do not really know which one has been placed there by Half Penny and won't know it until it attacks us."

This was a rather scary thought, but they hoped that somehow, Jacob and Amelia would be able to fight back.

"It's half-past five in the afternoon," Tom said, glancing at his watch. "I'd rather be in that cornfield in the daylight than at night."

"You see," Jacob said, "if we can stop the chief scarecrow, it will be easier to stop the others. Besides, it is the chief scarecrow that is hunting for the last two journals."

"But if the scarecrow comes to life at night, how shall we find it during the day?" Luna asked.

"Because during the day it is dead and as still and lifeless as any other normal scarecrow, stupid," Jacob said impatiently.

"You think you are so clever!" Tom chided him. "How shall we know which Half Penny's scarecrow is if it is disguised as a normal scarecrow in the daylight? At night, we can easily recognise it when it comes to life but then it will be deadly at night. What if it attacks us?

Remember, Half Penny almost killed you in the ruined house in the Mirror Dimension?"

"He didn't almost kill me!" Jacob snapped. "I fought back and left him choking with smoke in his eyes!"

"I would have loved to see that," Jack said. "Nothing pleases me than seeing somebody beat that creep at his own game."

He had had nightmares for weeks after the incident last year and still preferred to be with the others when he was outdoors. Half Penny had proven to be a remarkable force – one who could destroy half a city, even if the authorities thought it was a kids' fairy tale. They were faced with the responsibility of saving a city, and everyone thought they were crazy kids with an overactive imagination. But the massacre had proven that these monsters like Half Penny were extremely dangerous and deadly, and not just a fairy tale.

"So do we go or do we wait?" Luna asked impatiently.

"I have an idea," Jack said.

"What?"

"Let's go through the cornfield and let Luna point out the scarecrows she knows. The scarecrows that were not originally there must have been planted there by Half Penny and must be waiting for night to come so they can start terrorising people."

"Jack, that's genius!" Sera said admiringly.

"That's an excellent idea, Jack," Jacob agreed.

Jack beamed. He had been outshined often by Tom, Eliot and Jack and it was good to come up with a great idea. Why, even little Amelia made him feel helpless, considering how much power she possessed.

"Only one problem," Luna said. "It's a great idea, but I don't think I know every scarecrow that was originally in the cornfield. But at least we can cross out the ones I do know."

Chapter 8
WEIRD STUFF

Over the next three days, the group would split into two teams and some would be in the treehouse and some at Luna's place, but sometimes they all would be at Luna's. The farm was such an exciting place. Besides, it seemed that the farm may hold the mystery to the scarecrows, or at least a part of the mystery.

The group were gathered inside Luna's parents' house again. They could hardly concentrate on watching TV or doing much, because they were thinking about their adventure that night. Would they really be able to identify the scarecrows that were connected to Half Penny? Would they be able to identify the leader of the scarecrows that Half Penny had sent? And once they did, what would they do?

"We would have to rely on you and Amelia, Jacob," Tom said as soon as Luna's mother stepped out.

It was then that a news bulletin came on TV and they all turned to watch.

As the group looked in concern at each other, the newscaster's voice came to their ears. Twelve people had died that day and there were blurred images because some of the images could not be shown to the viewers. The newscaster said that many of these people had died as a result of blood loss and there was a lot of blood gushing from their heads. He also said that some had severed heads, and that these were scenes from the Halloween massacre. The group was however more worried that if someone told the Mayor about Jacob and the books, something terrible would happen. What would happen to Jacob – and the others? Would they be held responsible for everything that had happened if all the events were traced back to them?

Luna's mum dropped her cup of tea in shock and it shattered to a thousand pieces, spilling hot tea all over Luna's dad, who yelled in pain.

"What is going on?" Luna's mum spoke in a shocked voice. "You see why children should not be out there all alone? There is something very weird going on! Do you remember what happened to you on Halloween, Luna?"

The others knew that they could not tell Luna's parents what was going on. Luna's parents would not believe them, and even if they did, what could they do?

The next morning, when they were left alone to play a game that evening, the others decided that they could not go out to the cornfield tonight.

Later on that night, everyone was asleep except Jacob, so he got dressed and went for a walk in the field. When he walked out of the door, he used his dark magic fire as a torch. As he looked at the moon as he was floating in the air and was looking at the photo he still had in his pocket, he was sad for some reason about it.

Just then, he saw that the there was a light coming from afar in a nearby farm, so he went to investigate the mysterious light. It was coming from what seemed like a little house within the farm. For some reason the, farm seemed abandoned – as if people had lived there but no longer did. When he got there, he knocked on the door but no one answered. Then Jacob heard a sound that made him freeze.

Someone was digging in the moonlight!

He crept to the corner of the house and saw a figure that seemed to be doing some gardening. It seemed like a frail, old woman, but in the moonlight, he could only see her silhouette. Jacob, because of his powers, was very brave. When he got near the frail figure, he saw that now, it was very still but had turned into a scarecrow!

He went back to the little house's door. Suddenly, the strange light turned off, so he phased through the wall to investigate more, but didn't speak because he had a suspicious feeling that he wasn't alone and that something was wrong.

Then, he suddenly heard a glass fall on the floor, but that was just the beginning. He then saw a creaking door open slightly and saw a light coming out of the door. He went to investigate, but when he got there, he found the bleeding corpses of the people who had lived in the little house. There was a grave behind them, and he could hear a voice saying his name and that he was going to die!

When Jacob saw this, he was very shocked and spooked. Just then, the lights started turning green and flashing on and off crazily fast while making thunderous banging sounds. Something grabbed him by the shirt and threw him back against a plastic chair. He went crashing backwards as the chair toppled, and then again, he was grabbed by the front of his shirt. Before he was thrown down the stairs, he managed to have a glimpse of a scarecrow dressed in a torn black shirt and a hat that was full of feathers. He also noticed that it had a face that looked like a skull with empty eye sockets. The next thing he knew, he was rolling down the stairs.

He must have passed out temporarily. When he opened his eyes, he saw the scarecrow's silhouette at the top of the stairs. He summoned all his power and threw an energy blast at it as a way of fighting back, but all it did was throw it against the wall.

Jacob stood on his feet, and then panting ran upstairs with his hands burning with a purple flame and ready for a fight. The lights began to flash again and make sounds as he was pinned down to the floor by the scarecrow. It crawled over him and growled with rage.

While he was wondering what power or trick he could use against such a powerful creature, it suddenly disappeared. He lay there, wondering how it could disappear like that. As he got up, Half Penny appeared in a vision of the Mirror Dimension while he was playing the piano in a creepy tone that made Jacob shiver.

He said to Jacob, "Hello, Jacob. How do you like the surprise I told you about the other day? I told you it was going to be a nightmare of a summer for you." He cackled. "Now listen, tomorrow a mystery will be calling you and the others, so wait," said Half Penny, his voice echoing.

Just then, Jacob teleported back to the farm but decided to go for a quick fly around Dark Woods to clear his head. As he was flying over Dark Woods, he went to the treehouse to see how it was going but everyone was asleep and he could see that they had been trying to figure out Half Penny's plan – but all they'd been able to find was that his main goal was unknown. But they knew he must be planning something really big this time.

Then he heard footsteps behind him and saw that Amelia was behind him.

"Hello Jacob. Are you okay? I can see that you have seen what we have found out so far. I miss it when it was all of us in here in this treehouse."

Then Jacob said goodbye to Amelia as he ran at super speed back to the farm to help them if the scarecrow was hurting them, but when he got there, nothing was wrong – or so he thought.

When he saw a glow in the barn and went inside, he saw that Luna was there, sitting in sadness. Jacob sat next to her and tried to speak to her, wondering what the problem was.

Jacob spoke into Luna's mind, "Luna, can you tell what's wrong? Maybe I can help?"

Luna, sobbing, replied, "I'm just really scared of what's happening to us."

Jacob said, "Come on, it will be fine; we just need to be careful."

Luna quietly said, "Okay."

Just then, they heard a sound outside. As Jacob and Luna walked outside, they saw that someone was walking around at the edge of the trees where the forest joined the farm. So they went to investigate the strange sight.

As they ran as fast as they could, they found themselves in the centre of the cornfield. Now they assumed that it was probably just a hallucination.

Then Luna yelped and Jacob gasped as they saw a silhouette of a huge man. Then familiar laughter came to their ears, and they realised that it was actually a prank by Jack and Lucy in order to scare them. Jacob was not surprised because he could sense it from a mile away.

Jacob laughed sarcastically. "Very funny, guys."

Jack laughed and said, "Yeah, but we got you good."

Luna said, "Jacob, you've got to admit that was very funny."

Jacob scoffed. "Yeah, I guess."

Just then, the group heard something coming from behind them and they all decided to follow the strange sound to its source. As Jacob went into the forest to see the shadow he had just spotted, he shapeshifted into a frightening monster. He intended to get revenge on Jack and Lucy for pranking him. As Jacob loomed out of the bushes as a monster, the group fell down on their backs and screamed in shock.

Jacob, laughing and changing back to his normal self, said, "Oh my hell, you should have seen the look on your faces. Jack, when you screamed like that, you sounded like a baby girl."

Everyone sighed.

Chapter 9
THE FAKE JOURNAL

"I have a secret," Jacob whispered to Tom. "I want to trap Half Penny. He won't know what hit him. But I don't want all of us going out there. You see, I have a fake journal that would harm Half Penny if he opened it. But I don't want him to know I'm watching. If all of us go to the woods, we'll probably cause such a commotion that he'll know we are there. So you and I can go."

"But how will you attract Half Penny's attention? Do you intend to find him and hand over the journal?"

"Of course not. I want to go out there and bury the journal and make sure he knows where I buried it."

"Okay. I'm still wondering how you'll attract his attention so he can know where you hid the journal."

"A lamp. I've come to learn that if you walk around with a lamp out there, Half Penny will come investigating. Also, a lamp can reveal the portals that will take you from the ordinary woods to the Mirror Dimension."

"I see. Okay, let's go," Tom said. "But be careful in case Half Penny surprises you. He has done it before."

So the two snuck out and were gone before anyone knew what was happening. It was nearly 8 PM, and the scarecrows would be alive and haunting the farm and the woods, and moving around in the Mirror Dimension.

Once they had come to a certain spot deep inside the woods, Jacob whispered, "I've decided to light the lamp and also start a fire here.

That should attract Half Penny's attention. He might bring some scarecrows along to investigate. Now, start digging."

"Is this why you called me? So I can help you to dig?" Tom asked with a smile.

He was rather scared, though. Jacob might have powers, but there was always danger looming.

"Yes," Jacob said and grinned. "We are going to bury this polythene bag here. Don't look, but I think our friend is already creeping in the background trying to investigate. Quick, bury the bag."

A lamp and a fire. What an idiot, Half Penny thought. You don't go into the woods and start a fire in the night. There would be monsters creeping about in the woods, camouflaged by the tall grass. They would do anything for Half Penny, and considered obeying his commands as their greatest honour, and who were so good at tracking and hunting that they could get to within ten feet of Jacob before he even realised he had company.

The most interesting thing that happened, though, was that Jacob made a mark on a nearby tree and then began to dig. He buried the polythene bag with the fake journal and could not help chuckling to himself.

Half Penny made a mental note of the tree and the surroundings. Then he watched. The fire had only been burning for twenty minutes when Jacob found himself surrounded by five scarecrows holding daggers and clubs. One of the eerie scarecrows reached out its bony skeleton arm and smashed the club on Jacob's head. He fell like a sack of beans, and Half Penny began to drag him away, telling the two scarecrows to open the bag – he would be back. Tom watched, scared, hiding behind a tree.

The two scarecrows pulled out the polythene bag, opened it and then found themselves engulfed in flames. Their horrible screams would haunt Tom for days. They collapsed in a mass of burning clothes and bones.

Tom turned and ran.

Only Tom knew where Jacob had buried the fake journal before Half Penny took him away, so only he could take them there.

"If I find the spot," he said. "But if I find the two peculiar tree trunks that have no leaves and seem to have been burnt black in a fire, I will be able to find it."

"We can't all go," Luna whispered. "My parents will know immediately. So perhaps only two or three of us should go."

It was decided that Tom, Jack, Eliot and Luna would go. Lucy and Amelia had gone back home and Amelia had decided to sleep inside the treehouse she loved so much while Lucy spent the night in her bed. The funny thing was, if Lucy opened her window she could talk to Amelia as she lay in her treehouse bed. Amelia would have gone to her own home (where she lived with Jack and Sera as an adopted child), but with Jack away, she decided to stay at Lucy's that night.

So it was that midnight found them at the place Half Penny had visited. Tom knew where it was by the features and landmarks and he was able to lead them there. The spot was about half a mile into the woods from the edge.

"That's the tree," Tom said, pointing. "This is where he buried it."

"What's that?" Luna lifted the lamp and then gasped. It was a skull hung on a post. At the bottom of the post lay a skeleton, but it was the jacket that chilled their bones. That jacket belonged to Jacob.

"Jacob! Half Penny killed him!" Lucy whispered, her breath whistling through her teeth. "Come on, dig!"

They began to dig.

"Keep your eyes open, Luna," Eliot said. "Tom and I will dig."

Luna and Eliot had too much on their minds to start asking Tom how he knew the exact spot.

Finally, Tom pulled out the small polythene bag that Jacob had buried. Inside the polythene bag was the fake journal Jacob had shown them – the one he had said he would use to trick and punish Half Penny.

"Don't open that!" Tom urged. "Half Penny must have buried it again. When the scarecrows tried to open it, a flame jumped out and they died screaming."

"I don't want to burn to death," Luna said hastily, returning the book into the bag.

Just then, there was a gurgling sound and one of the scarecrows stood there, a lamp in his hand, frozen, an arrow sticking out of his back. Then he crashed to the ground face-first like a lifeless log.

Luna screamed involuntarily.

"Go! Run!"

In their haste, they had no time to bury the bag again. They did not see who had shot the scarecrow.

"You see that? There's a horse running after us!" Eliot gasped.

The lamp's light showed only a horse behind them. As they paused to look, an arrow came flying from the horse's direction and missed the lamp by six inches. They turned and stumbled again. Eliot tripped on a root and went down, but Tom and Luna kept running. This was an "every man for himself" situation.

They came to the edge of the woods and raced towards the path that would lead them towards the town. But they had to walk along the edge of the woods until they came to that path, because the ground here was set like a cliff.

There seemed to be no sound from the woods. It was as if they had imagined the rider-less horse and the shooter.

"I was so scared at seeing a horse without a rider chasing us that I forgot to use my spell power," Jack panted.

"That won't work," Luna gasped.

The Fake Journal

They planned to find the path that would lead them to where the farm was, near the ancient oak at the town's edge that cast a large shade by day and a mysterious shadow by night.

They walked on for about three-hundred yards, where they had to move in through the grass, trees and shrubs.

"Be quiet," whispered Jack. "As little noise as possible. That riderless horse really scared me. Do you think that's one of Half Penny's tricks?"

"Look at that little valley ahead. I know a place like that, but it's more like a little hill. We are in the Mirror Dimension. That rider-less horse and that scarecrow was in the Mirror Dimension too."

They heard the breaking twigs, and then turned and saw that horse again, racing towards them. They dashed off, but in her haste, Luna fell headlong into a ditch.

Tom and Jack pulled her out, and then they heard the sound of laughter coming from the direction of the horse.

"A laughing horse?" Eliot gasped.

They must have lost their way and gone in circles, because they found themselves where the dead scarecrow lay, the arrow still in his back. The lamp was still on, and they could see the charred bodies of the scarecrows that had tried to open the fake journal and gone up in flames.

Again, they heard the sound of breaking twigs and the sound of a horse's neigh.

"Tom! Jack!" a voice called. It was Jacob's voice. Just like the laughter, it came from the direction of the horse.

As the horse got closer to the lamp's light, they saw Jacob sitting on the horse!

"Did you forget I could be invisible when I chose to be?" Jacob asked. "It was funny to see you running away from the horse with an invisible rider."

"How dare you?" Luna snapped. "You scared us out of our wits!"

"That's a nasty prank, Jacob," Jack said, not amused at all.

"Sorry," Jacob said, and patted the horse. They seemed to have become friends.

"I'll call the horse Penny. Do you think I should take it with me?"

"But is it an ordinary horse? I would be terrified of a horse that roams around the Mirror Dimension," Luna said.

"Jacob, your fake journal killed those two scarecrows with a flame of fire!" Tom reminded him. "I saw that before Half Penny knocked you out and took you away. Your fake journal is powerful too and can be used to trick the scarecrows."

"Not anymore," Jacob shook his head. "Half Penny now knows that the journal can only harm the scarecrows and other monsters, and he will not allow them to open it."

"Yes, but he doesn't have it," Jack pointed out. "We can still use it to trick other scarecrows into opening it when we come across them."

"If Half Penny doesn't warn them first," Jacob said doubtfully. "It's Half Penny I wanted to open it, you see. Before he knew the trick, he would have been on fire himself."

"You'll have to think up another trick then," Luna told him.

Jacob nodded. Then he gaped. "Where's the horse gone?"

"I told you he was no ordinary horse," Luna said.

They walked back, taking the fake journal with them. If Half Penny told the other scarecrows about it, Jacob would have to come up with new tricks. The fake journal's secret was out of the bag.

"So what next?" Luna asked.

"Let's sleep on it," Jack suggested.

Chapter 10
MORE SCARES

The next morning was a rainy and stormy day and the kids were all huddled up around a fireplace at Luna's house. The tempestuous thunderstorm ravaged the neighbourhood. Its loud rumble made the kids shiver and huddle closer together. A strong gust of wind swept across the cornfield, the entire farm and the neighbourhood.

"Luna, tell us a horror story," begged Amelia with her irresistible puppy eyes.

"But I do not know any horror stories," replied Luna.

"Come on, Luna, you moved here from a small town in the middle of nowhere. I am sure there are some freaky stories you could tell us from your hometown," Jack added.

"Haven't you all experienced enough horrors in Dark Woods to want to listen to more?" teased Jacob.

"You know what, if everyone wants a story, I will give you one," Luna said, and started narrating her story.

"This is more of a scary experience than a horror story. When I was in kindergarten, my mother took to me upcountry to visit my grandparents out in Creeks Valley. They lived up in the mountains and their home was surrounded by trees. I had never been to a forest, so seeing so many trees together was quite something. I was excited to see my grandparents in person for the first time and I remember I couldn't contain my excitement that day.

"A few hours after arriving, I was shown to what would be my room for my short stay there. My mother told me that used to be her old room. She took the guest room. It had been a very pleasant day up until it was time to sleep. I was troubled nearly all night by a terrible nightmare. In my nightmare, there was this faceless, ghostlike figure who was out to get me. What was scarier was that despite my efforts to run away, I was stuck in the same spot.

"I remember waking up with a sudden jerk. But my nightmares followed me. That night, I saw a shadowy figure emerge from behind the big purple curtains in my room. The room was pitch black and the figure moved stealthily. I could tell he was tall and quite hairy. He dropped to the ground and I watched in horror as he crawled towards me. I let out a blood-curdling scream – enough to wake up dead bodies. Everyone in the house heard me and ran into my room. The moment my mother switched on the lights, the figure disappeared!"

"Hey kids," Luna's father casually said as he entered the room.

The kids all screamed in unison.

"Dad! You shouldn't scare us like that!" Luna was the first to speak.

"I almost jumped out of my skin!" Amelia added.

"What do you mean?" Luna's dad asked, confused, "I only greeted you, and it's nearly midday!"

"Luna was telling us a creepy story; that is why everyone is on edge," Jacob explained.

"Is it about the creepy scarecrow outside? I could have sworn I saw it moving someday but no one here believed me when I said it," Luna's father said casually while pouring himself a hot cup of coffee.

They all stared at him, shocked. How did he know about the scarecrows?

As he left, the group looked at each other with a worried look plastered on their faces. They all knew about how creepy and wild the scarecrow could get and they were instantly concerned. Had the scarecrow attacked Luna's father? This was a question that lingered in their mind but no one dared to voice it. Asking outright would mean they knew something about the scarecrow and would just generate more questions that they could not answer. Worse still, if Luna's father started getting suspicious, he would figure out everything and this could put him in danger.

"Do you think he knows? Should I erase his memories?" Jacob asked quietly.

"No! Absolutely not!" Luna said with conviction.

She realised she had raised her voice, so she added in a much lower tone, "We do not know the consequences of erasing one's memories, and I will not have you mess with my father's memory. Suppose he forgets even who I am or that I asked him to get me a new bike and a laptop? I am pretty sure he doesn't know anything. If he did, he wouldn't let it go. He's like a dog with a bone; once he smells something, he never puts it to rest. The way he casually brought it up makes me believe there is nothing to it."

The group took her word for it and easily let the matter slide. By this time, the storm had significantly reduced. Jack suggested that they play board games to pass time until they could all go out. They started with chess; everyone knew Luna was the queen of chess and, like always, she won. But the second time Luna realised that she had met her match as Jacob and then Amelia won.

"Are you two using your powers to win?" Tom asked Jacob and Amelia suspiciously.

"Maybe, maybe not," Jacob said with a wink.

"This is not fair," moaned Lucy, "You three will win every time if we keep playing."

Luna chuckled. "Okay, okay, you can all pick another game."

They settled on playing Monopoly. Even with Monopoly, they had a star – Jacob. But today, Jacob's mind was elsewhere. The competition was mainly just between him and Amelia, who was equally good – or who was using her powers.

However, this day, Jacob was doing quite poorly in the game. It was like his head was not even in it. The others could tell that something was bothering him. Luna could not shake the feeling that it had something to do with the picture of Jacob and a strange girl. Until now, he had refused to speak about the photo, and the others were now concerned.

"Hey Jacob, are you okay?" Luna asked.

"Yeah I'm… I'm fine… why… why do you ask?" Jacob stuttered.

"It is just that you seem preoccupied, and your head is not in the game. We are concerned about you," Luna replied.

"I am okay, guys, I am just feeling a little flushed," Jacob replied. Then he closed his eyes for a brief moment and then opened them and made such a sudden movement that the Monopoly board nearly fell off the table.

"You look like you have just seen a ghost!" Jack added.

"I said I'm okay! Geez, leave me alone!" Jacob said before walking out in a fit of rage.

It was now evident that Jacob was not okay. The other sat in stunned silence, not really comprehending why Jacob was acting like that.

"I really don't like this new side of Jacob. I just wish he could talk to us about whatever is bothering him." Amelia was the first to speak.

"Let us just cut him some slack. He is clearly going through something. As good friends, we should try to be there for him however we can," Luna answered.

"How can we be there for him if he doesn't want us to?" Jack wondered out loud

"Jacob is a very proud person; he will talk to us when he is ready," Amelia said, and turned her attention to the game.

Luna stood up to go pour herself a cup of coffee to drive out the cold. Jack also decided to get some. From where they stood, they could see Jacob sitting outside on a bench amidst the storm. He had used a force field to stop himself from getting wet. He just sat there alone, staring at the countryside. Jack and Luna looked at each other and their eyes communicated what they wanted to do without them saying it out loud. Luna put the pot of coffee down and together they walked out.

Luna and Jack went to Jacob and sat down next to him. Jacob was startled at first, but then he realised he could use some company. He extended the force field over them to cover them from the storm. They could still feel the cool breeze against their faces. Luna was glad she had worn a sweater because the force field could not protect them against the freezing temperature.

"Nice weather, isn't it?" It wasn't, but Luna said that for lack of something better to say.

"It's alright," Jacob replied absentmindedly.

"Do you think it will continue like this for the rest of the evening?" Jack asked.

"I hope not," Luna quickly replied.

Truth be told, she was not a big fan of the cold weather. Jacob on the other hand seemed to enjoy cold weather, so she tried to look like she was not dying to get back into the house. The trio sat there silently, each person lost in their own thoughts. Luna was the first to break the ice.

"Can I ask you something, Jacob?"

"Sure, go ahead," Jacob answered.

"Can you tell us who that girl next to you in the photo is?" Luna asked.

"Wh… why… why do you want to know?" Jacob stammered.

They were in freezing weather but he could have sworn he felt sweat run down his spine. Luna always made him a little uncomfortable. She was very straightforward and her piercing blue eyes always made him feel like she could read him like a book. With the others, he could simply ignore them, but she made it hard to just ignore her because she was staring at him straight in the eyes the whole time.

Jacob felt cornered and started to get a little paranoid. Not sure of what to do, he decided to turn invisible to avoid further questioning.

"Oh my goodness! Did he just vanish?" Luna asked, stupefied.

"Yep, he just did!" Jack replied.

"Wow... I can't believe him. What could be so secret that he can't talk about it with his friends?" Luna wondered

"Well, what did you expect, that he was going to tell you just because you asked nicely? I've known Jacob much longer than you have. I can tell you one thing for sure. He does not like to be pressured into things, and you intimidate him a little. Just let him talk to us when he feels ready," Jack advised her.

Luna could not help but feel terrible after what Jack had just said. She felt responsible for Jacob feeling that he had no choice but to turn invisible. And who knew what could happen to him out there without his friends? With Half Penny still on the loose, no one was ever really safe and they were safer as a group.

This situation reminded her of an experience back in her hometown. A girl in the same class as one of her cousins suddenly went missing. The police were informed within 24 hours and they launched a massive search for her. In the ensuing investigations, it was revealed that the girl was constantly bullied in school. She was picked on by other older kids who always took her lunch. The girl had reported to the administration once, but nothing much was done; the girls who picked on her were only given detention for a day. The bullying got worse from there. They punished her for telling on them and promised her that they would do worse if it happened again.

The girl felt so lost and unseen. While many asked questions, no one ever did anything to help. So when she had had enough, she just thought her best option would be to disappear. After all, no one would care. Luckily enough, nearly everyone cared. Her classmates worked overtime with the police to help find her. They organised search parties and made all kinds of posters for a missing person. Within a week, she was found. She could not believe all the effort that went into finding her, so she mattered after all. The bullies were suspended indefinitely and for the first time, she had friends.

"Luna! Earth to!" spoke Jack.

Luna broke off from her thoughts. She had spaced out thinking about the story of that girl. She felt somehow guilty and responsible for Jacob's disappearance. If she hadn't pushed the matter, he would still be here. She couldn't forgive herself if anything happened to him.

"We have to do something, Jack! Half Penny is still out there and you know he preys on the vulnerable. Jacob is in a vulnerable position right now. We have to get him back!" Luna said hysterically.

"Personally, I think Jacob can take better care of himself than any of us can, including Amelia," Jack said. "But if you are so worried, perhaps we should do something. Do you think we should ask for help from the others?" he asked, concerned.

"No... No, I don't want to cause panic among the others. We have to try and find him ourselves. I just wish there was a way to find someone who doesn't want to be found," Luna mourned.

At that moment, Jack remembered a certain spell he was taught by Jacob to find someone who was lost. Jacob and Amelia had read about this spell in the journal. Jacob taught Jack this spell as a safety precaution in case Half Penny was in the real world and they needed to save someone.

"I know how we can get him back!" Jack shouted with excitement. "Jacob taught me a spell you can use to locate someone."

He fished out a letter from his pockets and said the magic words "Insodia Denas Nightuom Trackious Insodias!" and a blue, ghost-like mist footprint appeared out of the ground. They followed the footprint, which led them deeper and deeper into the forest. Luna was concerned about how further they needed to go but she could not turn back at this point. The footprints led then to where Jacob was. They saw him sitting on a certain big stone and throwing rocks absentmindedly.

Luna ran up to him and hugged him tightly.

"Oh Jacob, you do not know how glad I am to see you!" Luna said.

"We are so sorry for prying into your personal life. We just wanted to help," Jack added

"Sorry if we hurt your feelings. Please forgive, Jacob," Luna said.

Chapter 11
THE SCARECROWS

Seeing how remorseful his friends were made Jacob feel bad about how he had reacted. He wanted to tell his friends about the photo but he just felt that it was not the right time. However, the longer he waited, the more anxious they got. He had created such a big mystery around the photo that everyone was expecting it to be some mind-blowing, life-changing piece of information.

"I am sorry too, guys, I didn't mean to scare you like that," Jacob said.

"No, it's okay, don't be sorry, we were wrong too," Luna said empathetically.

"About the photo, I am just not ready to talk about that now. But I am making a promise now, that when the time feels right, I will reveal everything. I just ask that you be patient with me and not bring it up often. When I am ready, I will talk about it myself," Jacob said.

"We promise not to bring it up again," Luna said with a smile.

"Pinky swear?" Jacob asked with a childish grin.

"Pinky swear," Jack and Luna both replied, smiling.

Meanwhile, back in the Mirror Dimension, Half Penny was enjoying messing a little family about on vacation. The family of four had rented a small, two-storey cabin at the edge of the woods and had planned to stay there for a week enjoying the countryside. It had been a long time since the family had gotten together so they hoped this would be a good bonding experience. The dad and the son had gone out fishing while the young girl, Claire, stayed behind with her mother.

The mother and the young girl were putting away clothes in their rooms upstairs when Half Penny caused all the doors downstairs to start banging continuously. The mother and girl were so shocked that they ran downstairs to see what was wrong. To their disbelief, no one was downstairs, and there was no wind blowing against the doors to cause them to bang like that.

"What on earth could be wrong with these doors?" the mother shouted.

"I don't know, mum, maybe we didn't lock the doors well," answered Claire, the little girl.

The mother went and locked the doors. Meanwhile, Half Penny was watching and laughing hysterically. The terrified look on their faces was so satisfying.

For the next two hours, he would continue to mess with them in many different ways. He would cause faceless shadows to appear and disappear all across the house, especially to the little kids. Little Claire was convinced that she was being haunted.

"Should we leave?" Claire's mother said to her husband. "This place is so creepy."

"No one's getting hurt," Claire's father said obstinately. "Besides, what would my friends say if they heard I had run away from a house when I was on vacation. They will be laughing at me for years. I paid for a week's vacation, and that's what we are going to have, ghosts or no ghosts!"

At 13 years old, Claire had heard so many stories about ghosts and was sure what she was seeing were ghosts. She would cry to her mum but her mother kept reassuring her that it was just her paranoia causing her to see things.

While Half Penny was not physically hurting this family, the emotional and mental torture was just as worse. It was not until the mother experienced a bizarre and creepy incident that made her believe there were some truths in her children's allegations.

She woke up that afternoon before everyone else and went downstairs to prepare breakfast. As she was getting the coffee pot ready, she heard the eerie sound of a child crying outside. She walked to the window and peeped to see who that was. There on the trail leading up to their cabin was a small girl in bloodied white clothes. On her hands, she was carrying an Annabelle doll with the eyes gorged out. She had blood coming from one side of her lips and was making this eerie sound, like an animal in pain. The girl had an unnatural stare. The mother was so shocked that she felt paralysed on the spot.

She gathered all the strength she could to call out to her husband, who woke up quickly to see what could have been wrong. Immediately as the husband joined her at the window than the girl disappeared.

That was the last straw for this family. They moved out by 6 PM that very day, much to the pleasure and delight of Half Penny. He could not wait to torture those teenagers who had outsmarted him several times before – especially Jacob and Jack. He still believed that Jack could set him and his friends free, and that Jacob was a problem that should be taken care of before he caused mayhem in the Mirror Dimension or used his journals to destroy everything. Half Penny was determined to stop those teens once and for all.

He quickly switched to the Mirror Dimension's version of the farm, and with a very evil smirk on his face. It was almost time for the trap he was setting for them on the farm.

"Looks like the next move is like a game of chess, and the next move is prince takes knight and eventually checkmate," Half Penny said to himself with an evil grin, and then he started laughing maniacally.

Back in the house, Amelia had was bored out of her mind with the others gone. Lucy was not much of a board game enthusiast and she was seated in front of the TV, flipping through channels. Monopoly was no fun without someone to play with, so Amelia decided she would go home instead. As the only other kid with powers (unless there was somebody else whose powers were a secret), she also created a force field protection from the light storm that was still outside and walked home.

Lucy found a channel that mildly interested her – The Discovery Channel. She loved animals, but not the aggressive ones. Lucy preferred the less intimidating and adorable domesticated animals like cats, puppies, dogs, rabbits or even birds. Predatory animals scared her, and at that moment, the channel was showcasing a feature story about the predatory nature of the hyenas. She did not want to watch such violent and ugly scenes alone, but for some weird reason, she was fixated on it. She knew Luna's parents were upstairs so that gave her some semblance of security.

As Lucy watched, something about the hyenas after feeding, with their mouths all bloodied and a wild look on their faces, gave her some strange déjà vu. She could have sworn that once in passing, the scarecrow on Luna's farm had given her the same look. It was just for a split second and then it looked normal again, but she could still remember how her heart had stopped in that second. She had quickly brushed it off as just part of her wild imaginations and blamed it on fatigue, but now she was not so sure.

What if she had really seen something? What if that was Half Penny messing with her, she wondered to herself. With everything they had witnessed since the strange happenings on Halloween, everything was plausible. She knew Half Penny would always find ways to mess with them since they presented a threat in stopping him. The more she watched, the more anxious she got. She mastered all her strength to switch off the TV. She shook herself as if she was shaking all the bad spirits off of her.

Lucy decided to go lay down in Luna's bedroom as she waited for the others to come back. As cosy as Luna's bed was, she did not sleep a wink. She kept tossing and turning on the bed. She could not get that image of the hyena feeding out of her mind. It was the semblance that it bore to the scarecrow outside that bothered her even more.

To ease her mind, she stood up and went to the bedroom window to look out at the scarecrow. There it was, looking all menacing while flapping its supposed arms from side to side. Its human-like features were pretty unnerving. It was designed to look like a person to provide maximum protection to the cornfield.

Suddenly, Lucy heard a loud noise behind her like something big had fallen. She quickly turned to look but there was nothing there. The room was the same way it had been.

That's strange, she thought to herself.

She thought maybe it was Luna's parents who had dropped something. She turned her attention back to the scarecrow and received the shock of her life. The scarecrow was no longer there in its holder!

"What the hell!" Lucy said out loud. "It was there just a second ago!"

As if that wasn't enough, the lights suddenly started going on and off on their own. They were not even glowing in their normal colour; they were all glowing green. Lucy was too stunned to even move; her heart was beating so fast that she felt she could hear her own pulse rate. What freaked her out even more is that out of nowhere, the rumble of a thunderclap was felt all across the room. Crack! That was all she heard before a lightning bolt struck through the sky.

Lucy closed her ears and started to wail because all these happenings were so unnatural. Despite there being a storm in the morning, the sky was now clear and it had even stopped raining. She was moving back towards the door while closing her ears when she felt she bumped into something hard. She slowly turned to see what it was and lo and behold, it was the scarecrow! Lucy let out the loudest scream of her life. If it was an audition for *Scream Queens*, she should have gotten the lead role.

She immediately turned to run after her initial shock but just as she was about to take a step, the scarecrow grabbed her and what happened immediately after was a blur.

Luna's parents were the first to be alarmed by Lucy's scream. Luna's mother, who was touching up her face in the bedroom, was so startled that she dropped and broke the mirror. She quickly jumped over the broken glass and ran in hot pursuit with Luna's father right behind her. They knew their daughter had left earlier with two of the boys but believed both the girls were still in the house. The noise could either be from Lucy or Amelia.

"Lucy! Amelia! What's wrong?" Luna's mother shouted in panic.

"Girls! What is it?" Luna's father shouted, getting ahead of his wife and opening Luna's room. To their shock, there was no one in the room. "Where could they have gone to? There is nobody here!" Luna's father said in shock.

"I could have sworn the noise came from here," Luna's mother said, equally surprised.

"But there is no way anyone could have left the room in those few seconds it took us to run here!" Luna's father added.

"This is very strange. Somebody had to have screamed that loudly, it was a cry of distress – but where are they?" Luna's mother wondered aloud.

She had barely finished saying that sentence when strange happenings started to occur in their daughter's room. The lights started going on and off and were glowing green. And just like it happened to Lucy, a loud thunderclap was heard before a lightning bolt struck.

By this time, they were getting very spooked. This scene took them back to last year's Halloween when the lights were behaving in a similar way. Luna's mother was now getting very scared; she had never really reconciled everything that had happened during last year's Halloween and all the chaos that ensued.

As if things could not get any creepier, the scarecrow that was usually on their farm appeared right in front of them and roared.

"Aaaaaaaaaahhhhhh!" Luna's mother screamed in terror with all her might.

"What the…" Luna's father started.

Lucy ran out of the room towards the dark corridor, thinking that perhaps the scarecrow would not see her in the darkness. But just then, the lights came on and she realised she was standing in front of the mirror that stood on the wall of the little sink at the end of the corridor.

Lucy stared in horror as the mirror began to crack right in front of her eyes. She screamed.

"Lucy! What's going on?" her father yelled, and came running, followed by the others. They were just in time to see the mirror smash into little pieces on the floor, and then the light up on the ceiling went off.

"Get out!" Luna's father said urgently, but just then, they heard Luna's mother scream somewhere in the house.

They ran towards the kitchen, almost stumbling in the passage.

"What's going on, darling?" Luna's father panted.

"I saw something like a scarecrow standing in the doorway! Can you believe that? I was cooking. When I turned around, the knife I had been using was gone."

"Gone? A knife can't just disappear," her husband said.

"Neither do mirrors break by themselves," Jacob said. "It's Half Penny."

"Half what?" Luna's father asked. They had never mentioned Half Penny to the adults before.

There was no time to explain, however.

Chapter 12
THE NECKLACE

Back in the woods, Luna could not shake the feeling that something was not right back at home. Five minutes earlier, Jacob had heard a faint, distant scream.

"Did you hear that?" Jacob, who had a heightened sense of hearing, asked.

"What?" Luna and Jack asked in unison.

"That scream? You know what... never mind; it's probably nothing," Jacob said.

Despite Jacob's reassurance, Luna had grown restless. She wanted to tell the others that they should go back now, but for the first time in a while, they were having a good time. It was dark but the moonlight shone brightly. The stars were all out tonight; it was a beautiful sight to see. Jacob was not grumpy and even made a few dad jokes that had them in stitches. The trees and the nature around them offered a very cool breeze and a serene environment for them to hang out.

It was not until the second scream that they all heard that they got alarmed.

"Oh my God, I heard it this time!" Jack shouted.

"And I think it's coming from our farm!" Luna added.

With realisation, they all began to panic. They all took off to go and investigate.

As the group arrived at the house, they noticed that it was quiet, a little too quiet. All the lights were out; it was pitch black.

"Amelia! Lucy!" Jack called out.

"Mum! Dad!" Luna cried out.

She was now visibly worried and so were the others. It was clear to them that no one was home. Luna knew that it was so unlike her parents to leave the house unattended at this time of the night. Jack felt that her adopted sister Amelia would not go back home without him. Jacob on the other hand was sure Lucy would always wait for them before heading home. Besides, she was always scared of walking home alone.

"This is strange, guys, my parents always leave the security lights on soon as it starts to get dark. They would never switch it off until the light of day comes," Luna stated as she walked around the house to inspect.

"I also think it's very unlikely that both Amelia and Lucy left without waiting for us," Jack added.

"Guys! Guys!" Luna called out from her room. "Look at my room! I would never leave my room like this. The laundry basket is knocked over and all my dirty clothes are scattered on the floor. My nightstand has also been knocked over and the bedside lamp is broken!" Luna said in one breath.

"You are right, Luna, there seems to have been a struggle here. This doesn't look normal."

After establishing that something was indeed wrong, Jack and Luna got their flashlights out and turned them on. Jacob harnessed his powers and turned his hands and eyes purple. He also created fire with his hands for some light to guide them through the dark.

"Perhaps we should split up so we can cover more ground and hopefully find something useful about what happened here," Jacob suggested.

"Yes, sure, but we should search outside; there seems to be nothing in here. Maybe the clues are outside."

They all went outside and started looking for clues. As the group went in separate directions in the farm area, little did they know that they were playing right into the scarecrow's devious plans. It was his hope all along that the trio would separate and make it much easier for him to kidnap them. Divide and conquer.

"Yes, come on, little ones!" the scarecrow said to himself.

While Luna was walking, her necklace started to glow and growl, like it was trying to tell her something. Luna was so startled that she almost took it off and threw it away. It was then that she vaguely remembered Jacob saying he had once seen the necklace in a dream, which meant that it had to be special. She tried to relax and pay attention to whatever the necklace may have been signalling her to do. She was still staring at the necklace when she heard something coming from the barn. She walked slowly inside and saw that someone was just standing inside facing the wall.

"He... Hell... Hello, who are you?" Luna stammered, feeling scared.

"Hello sir, this is our farm; can I help you?" Luna added when she got no response.

The man did not move an inch nor respond. Luna began to approach him as her curiosity got the better of her. She placed her hand on his shoulder. The man suddenly made a quick turn and with a swift moment, stretched out a hand that felt like claws when it raked her hair. She jumped back with a squeal.

The man attacked her with a rage she had never seen before. One of her greatest fears in life was being attacked by a possessed person and it was all becoming a reality. She screamed in terror as the man threw her to the wall and she was knocked out cold. She could not remember anything after that vicious attack.

Jack, on the other hand, had taken his search to the cornfield. His first cause of concern and alarm was seeing that the scarecrows were off their holders. He instantly felt very scared; this meant that the scarecrows had come to life and were probably behind all the strange happenings that night.

While he was still trying to come to terms with this new realisation, he heard a scream coming from the barn. He rushed to investigate and when he walked slowly into the building, the light of his phone picked out the words on the wall written in dripping blood: "We're back!"

The message alone was enough to send Jack into distress, but the fact that it was also written in blood made it even more disturbing. Jack, who never had a strong stomach for disturbing things, started whimpering and he felt like he was about to get sick. He heard footsteps coming from outside and it instantly gave him a cold chill.

They are back! They are here for me, he thought to himself in panic.

Jack did not want to wait to see who or what that could be. He took off as fast as his feeble legs could carry him. He was moving at a hundred miles per hour when something grabbed his leg and tripped him over. He fell with a loud thud, cut his chin and started bleeding. He was still reeling from the pain of the fall when he was attacked by the scarecrow. He knew the scarecrows had come to life but he was still taken aback at seeing one like this. The scarecrow was dressed in tattered clothes and its skull had empty eye sockets. Usually, the scarecrows in the cornfield were made of stuffing.

The scarecrow growled at him and started dragging him to the barn while he screamed, "Noo! Not again! Don't send me back to the dark, noo!!"

Meanwhile, Jacob was wondering where his friends had disappeared to. Even though they had taken different directions, it had been nearly 20 minutes or more. They should have made their way back by now. He could not even see the light from their flashlights.

Maybe they found nothing and have gone back to the house, Jacob thought to himself.

He then decided to go check if the others had gone back to the house. He was still using his powers of light to help him navigate through the dark. He walked slowly into the house while being guided by the purple flames. Hardly had he made four steps into the house when he heard some noise coming from the study.

"Jack, Luna, is that you?" Jacob called out cautiously.

He did not get a response. Instead, there was more rattling and then, out of nowhere, he saw a man run out of the study. Jacob quickly followed him to investigate who it was and what he was doing in Luna's house.

As he followed the man, he noticed a piece of yarn or hay on the floor on the carpet near the study's doorway. He thought maybe it got stuck on Luna's or Jack's shoes when they came back in the house. This was proof to him that either Luna or Jack had to be in the house.

As he got near the study doorway, he felt a hard, blunt object hit him so hard in the head. The blunt force caused him to lose himself for a minute and before he could even recover, someone pushed him down the stairs. Thank goodness it was only a few steps, otherwise he would have been knocked out cold.

Jacob had a higher pain tolerance ever since was young, but somehow, getting these powers had heightened that tolerance. So as long as he did not pass out, he could withstand a little pain.

He opened his eyes enough to see the scarecrow surging forward to attack him. Without thinking, he released a lightning bolt at the scarecrow. The power surge threw the scarecrow against a wall and with the few seconds to spare while the scarecrow was down, Jacob gathered his strength and bolted out the door. This was the moment it hit Jacob that the scarecrow was the root of all the strange happenings that evening.

Chapter 13
TERROR ON THE FARM

The scarecrows had always been creepy but he never thought they would launch an attack against them. Somehow, he still felt that someone was driving the scarecrows to this aggressive behaviour. He could not wait to tell Luna and Jacob what had happened to him and that he finally knew who was behind everything.

"Jack! Luna! Guys, where are you?" Jacob shouted at the entrance of the house.

"Meelp… Maacob, meelp," eerie, muffled voices were heard saying.

"Hello… who said that?" Jacob asked. He had a heightened sense of hearing so despite the voices being distant, he could hear them.

"Meelp! Meelp!" the muffled voices continued.

Jacob was now certain that someone was trying to call out for help but, for some reason, could not articulate the words correctly. Maybe someone was trying to keep them silent and that is why their voices came out muffled.

It was at this point that it dawned on Jacob that his friends had been captured by this thing or by the man he saw earlier in the house. He then realised that he was facing his fears of losing everything he cared about. First Lucy and Amelia were gone and now Luna and Jack were missing. He was all alone.

"No, this cannot be happening!" he screamed out in frustration. "Lunaaaaaaa!" he yelled as he knelt on the ground. He released a purple energy wave that moved in one direction.

Jacob felt the wave and he knew it was trying to help him find his friends. He followed the direction of the wave and it led him upstairs to Luna's parents' bedroom. The moment he stepped into the room, he heard the muffled sounds more clearly. They were coming from the closet.

He used his super strength to pry the doors open. There on the floor of the closet were Luna and Jack, bound by a strong rope and gagged, which is why their cry for help came out muffled and sounded weird.

"Oh my God! Luna! Jack! Are you guys okay?" Jacob asked as he dropped on his knees to untie them. He started by removing the gag from both of them.

"Please untie us quickly before he comes back," Luna begged.

"Did he hurt you? Are you hurt?" Jacob asked them, concerned, as he continued to untie them.

"I just have a bad headache from when he threw me to the wall. My head still hurts," Luna said.

"I think I hurt my leg from when I tripped and fell," Jack added.

"I'm sorry, guys, we should have never split up. This would have never happened if we had all stuck together," Jacob apologised.

"It's not your fault, Jacob, we all unanimously agreed to split up," Luna said.

"Do you know that it is the scarecrow launching these attacks!" Jacob said in astonishment.

"Yes, we are aware. I suspected them when I noticed they were out of their holders," Jack said.

Jacob helped Luna and Jack up. Jack realised that he walked with a bit of a limp from falling. Luna needed a few minutes to steady herself because her head was buzzing.

"Do you both need some rest? I can go and check out the scarecrow in the barn myself if you don't feel up to it," Jacob said empathetically.

"No, I am now sure the scarecrow took my parents and our friends, so I am going too. I have to find out where it took them!" Luna said with determination.

"Me too. I also want to find out where our friends went. Besides, we said we are not going to split up again. We are stronger together," Jack added.

That said, the trio began to walk to the cornfield. Luna was feeling better after drinking a glass of water. Jack's legs only needed a bit of motion to get the blood flowing so he could walk well again. There was still a bit of pain in his hip bone but he braved the pain.

They heard footsteps fading in the cornfield so they rushed to investigate. As they ran, Luna lagged because she could not run as fast due to her head injury. One of the scarecrows grabbed Luna's feet and began to pull her back.

"Heeeelp! Heeelp! Jaaacob!" Luna screamed out loud.

Jack and Jacob were so shocked to turn and see Luna being dragged by a scarecrow. They quickly ran to her, got hold of her hands and started pulling.

"Get it off of me! Get it off me please, I don't want to be taken!" Luna cried hysterically.

But just then, somehow, Luna's necklace felt her emotions and sensed her distress. It started to glow brightly and released an energy blast. Everyone within a fifty-yard radius was propelled away, including the scarecrow. Luna could not comprehend what had just happened and how she was able to do that with the power of the necklace. Jack and Jacob quickly stood up and ran to Luna.

"How did you do that, Luna?" Jack asked, impressed.

"I cannot even explain it; all I know is that my necklace started glowing and released that energy blast!" Luna said in wonder.

"Luna, I once told the others that I've seen your necklace before… about 4 years ago in a dream. It glowed and had magic just like you just saw it do," Jacob explained.

"Wow! I mean, I have always known it was special but I never knew it had so much power!" Luna said in amazement.

"Soon, I'll be the only one left without special powers," Jack said, looking down.

"C'mon Jack, we are all special in our way. Everyone has that one thing they can do better than everyone else," Luna consoled him.

"Come on, guys, we need to keep moving; we do not have all the time. The others are still missing and we need to find them. Let us keep on looking," Jacob said.

They all stood up and continued the search. At that moment, they were all feeling pretty confident. Between Luna's newfound magical powers and Jacob's superpowers, they had enough strength to defeat the scarecrow.

They saw a fleeting shadow of a scarecrow and began chasing it. It was moving towards the barn. They chased it to the barn but when they arrived, there was no one there, almost like they were just following a shadow.

Luna noticed some new changes in the barn that had not been there before. One section had more hay than the other.

"Hey guys, this is a little strange. We always spread hay evenly across the barn but here, it looks like only one section has hay," Luna noted.

"You are right, Luna, it is almost as if someone is trying to hide something by putting all the hay in one place," Jack added.

The trio started removing the hay to see if there was anything hidden under it. To their surprise, there was a hole underneath! They started removing the hay faster and lo and behold, Luna's parents and Lucy were trapped underneath. Jacob used his super strength to help pull Luna's parents up, despite him being just a child. Jack and Luna helped Lucy out of the hole.

Lucy was very weak and disillusioned. She had been crying the whole time they were stuck in the hole. She was also claustrophobic so being stuck in a hole was her absolute worst nightmare. After this, she was going to need a lot of therapy just to be okay again.

"Mum! Dad!" Luna cried out as she hugged them in a warm embrace.

"Oh, baby! I am so glad to see you. I thought I was never going to see you again in my life," her mother cried.

"My only prayer was that you remained safe, even if we were gone," Luna's father said, joining in for a group hug.

Jacob and Jack tried to hold Lucy in an attempt to calm her down. She was still hysterical, despite being rescued.

"Guys, we have to move in case the scarecrows are still in the vicinity," Jacob said.

"You are right; the scarecrows have been checking up on us to see if we are still here. I am sure they are about to do their rounds," Luna's father added.

Jacob and Jack supported Lucy as they walked out of the barn with Luna and her parents following closely. As soon as they stepped out of the barn, the combine harvester turned on and started to drive towards them in an attempt to run them over. Looking keenly, they noticed it was being driven by the scarecrow.

"Guys, get behind me; I am going to try and create a force field to stop it!" Jacob shouted.

Everyone got behind him and Jacob created a force field to try and protect them from it. However, the strength of the scarecrow was starting to feel too strong for him. He could feel that he was about to lose the struggle.

"Stop the scarecrow! I can't hold it any longer!" Jacob shouted while grunting in pain.

Luna's father ran to try and stop the scarecrow. Jack ran to try and stop the combine harvester. It was moving with speed. He timed it with precision and then jumped on it to try and turn it off manually.

Luna's father picked up a large stick and started hitting the scarecrow. The scarecrow broke off its concentration on driving the combine harvester and turned its attention on Luna's father. It grabbed him by the collar and lifted him. On seeing this, Luna became so scared and worried. Her necklace started to glow and growl.

"Let him goooo!" Luna screamed, and immediately, her necklace released an energy blast that propelled everyone back.

The scarecrow let go of Luna's father and he immediately stood and ran to them. They all quickly ran back to the house and locked all the doors. The adrenaline rush was unlike anything Luna's mother had never experienced before. She had been there and had experienced everything with the others, but could not explain what had just happened. She had so many questions, but looking around, this was not the right time to ask.

"Lucy! Why was Amelia not with you? Was she taken to another place?" Jack asked, concerned for his sister.

"No, Amelia was not taken. She was so bored earlier with you guys gone that she went home," Lucy replied in a feeble voice.

"Oh, thank God!" Jack breathed a sigh of relief.

For the first time, he was grateful for his adopted sister's impatience. Besides, she would be with Sera back home. On many occasions, it was a reason for conflict between them, but today, her impatience had saved her from a traumatic event that would have scarred her for life.

"It looks like the scarecrows are retreating from the house. I can hear their footsteps moving away," Jacob announced.

"Do you think they are going back to their holders in the cornfield?" Jack asked.

"I cannot yet comprehend what happened here today, but what I know for sure is I am not still keeping those things in my field. If they are there tomorrow, they will all be cut down!" Luna's father declared angrily.

No one said a word. No one could blame him for feeling like that. The kids knew they had a lot to explain to Luna's parents, but right now, everyone was exhausted. Everyone retreated to their respective bedrooms to rest. Everything else could wait for the light of day.

But just then, the group heard footsteps coming from outside, and Jacob barricaded the walls and door with wood using his magic. He would lift the pieces of wood with his magic, shove them across the room, and pin them to the walls, windows, and doors. Everyone had to stay out of the way, lest they were pinned to the walls by the flying objects.

As soon as they were done barricading the walls and doors, thinking that they were now safe, the scarecrows started to break into the barn. They punched through the wood as if it was nothing. A punch into the wall and there was a big hole, a kick into the wall, and there was another hole.

They broke the barricades in seconds, charged at them, and started to attack. Furniture was hurled across the room, people ducked to avoid getting hit, but some were not so lucky as they got beat up by the scarecrows. They all fought against them with as much strength as possible, but the scarecrows seemed to be overpowering them. They were not going down without a fight, and when it seemed that all hope was lost, Luna came to the rescue and saved the day. She decided to use her magic.

She used her magic to lift an axe that stood at one of the corners of the house to chop off the scarecrow's head, scaring off the others.

"Jacob, duck!" shouted Luna.

"What?" Jacob asked.

"Duck!" Luna answered.

Jacob turned to look at Luna, only to see an axe flying across the room towards him. He understood what she meant and fell to the ground immediately to give way to the flying object. It flew straight toward the scarecrow he had been fighting and across its neck. A greenish, squishy liquid flew out of the chopped neck as the detached head bounced on the ground. The headless body fell to the ground and lay there motionless.

As they stood there looking at it and happy that they had won, the unbelievable happened. Unfortunately, the huge slash didn't even kill the scarecrow. They were taken aback as they watched the scarecrow that lay headless a few minutes earlier wake up and just put its head back on, twist its neck as if to lock it back in place like nothing had happened, and continue to attack them.

Chapter 14

A DEADLY DISCOVERY

When the group was busy fighting the scarecrows that were attacking them, they tried to throw a knife at Jack, but by good luck, Jacob saw it on time and used his telekinesis to stop him from being killed. The knife almost chopped Jack's head off, but luckily, it just scraped the side of his head. He was bleeding very badly, which meant that the cut was deep.

In the process of trying to protect Jacob using her magic, Jacob and Luna's magic somehow collided and caused an enormous energy shockwave that threw everyone to the ground and stunned the scarecrows temporarily. They all tried to stand up, groaning and rubbing their heads, trying to make sense of what had happened. They barely had time to even ask each other what had happened as the scarecrows surrounded them and had everyone cornered, ready to stab and slaughter each and every one of them.

Everyone screamed in terror and fear as they huddled together at the centre of the room. Jacob's eyes darted around the room, trying to find the book that had been thrown from his hands during the fight. He saw it, but his only problem was how to get to it.

Jack had seen Jacob look around and noticed his eyes land on the book. He immediately figured that he wanted the book.

"Hey, I shall distract them as you try to reach for the book?" Jack whispered.

"How will you do that?" Jacob asked.

"I will figure it out; just wait for the cue and make a run for it," Jack answered.

"Fine, hurry and don't get us killed," stated Jacob.

Jack started yelling at the scarecrows, which got them worked up. They started moving towards Jack, looking furious, and now that he had their attention, he figured it was the best time for Jack to pounce and grab the book.

"Now, Jacob!" Jack shouted.

Everyone seemed startled from the shouting, including the scarecrows. Before they could figure out what was going on, Jacob had dashed across the room and picked the book up in one scoop.

He perused through the pages hurriedly, trying to get to the page that had the story. Luckily, Jacob opened the scarecrow's story at the last minute, and it sucked them all back into its story, and he slammed the book tight. It was as if everyone was holding their breath, waiting for the worst to happen, because as soon as the scarecrows were sucked in and the book closed, they all let out a sigh of relief.

Jacob was the first to speak as he said while panting, "That was close. Is everyone okay?"

"Yeah, I'm okay," Jack answered.

"What in the world is going here?" Luna's mum and dad asked, looking very confused.

"Look, we can explain," Jacob answered.

He was not going to let them get mixed up in all that was happening, and so at that minute, Jacob used his powers to wipe their memories of that day and whatever had happened to them. They would not be able to remember what happened. The only problem was how to explain all the mess in the house. They were going to have to figure something out.

"Why are we here, and what happened? It looks as if a tornado passed through here," said Luna's mum, her eyes wandering around the house in confusion.

"You were going to check on the pigs and make a new scarecrow," Luna answered.

It was true; that was what she had intended to do before the scarecrows attacked them. She looked at her mother straight in the face. She did not want to go into detail as she would rather not endanger their lives by letting them find out the truth. They would not believe her anyway if she told them about what had happened during Halloween. Half Penny was very ruthless, and if he figured out that they knew he existed, he would come after them.

"And why is he bleeding?" she asked, pointing at Jack.

"Oh ma'am, it's just a small wound. I'll be okay," Jack said, but did not mention the scarecrows.

As Luna's parents walked away, Luna couldn't help but wonder what Jacob had done to her parents.

"What did you do to my parents?" Luna asked.

"I made them forget all that happened," Jacob answered.

"Are you sure it will work? And will it have any effect on them?"

"Ha ha ha, no, it won't have any effect on them, and yes, I am very sure it will work. They will not be able to remember a thing about today," Jacob laughed.

"You all put up a good fight today. I didn't think we would get out of that fight alive," Luna said.

"You are right. We all did," Jacob agreed.

"Did you see what happened when our powers collided?" Luna added, sounding very excited.

"Yes, it goes to show you how powerful we can be when we work together. We have the power and capability of getting rid of Half Penny for good," Jacob said.

Those words were barely out of his mouth when a strong wind started to blow. It was so strong that they had to hold on to whatever was near them to avoid being carried away. A portal then opened, and out of it appeared Half Penny.

"Do not think that just because you won the fight today and destroyed some of my scarecrows that you are even close to beating me. I will destroy you all. You can never beat me. Wait until you see what I have in store for you! I will kill you all!" Half Penny bellowed, and with those words, he disappeared into the portal and let out a loud, sarcastic laugh as the portal closed behind him.

Back in the Mirror Dimension, Half Penny watched them from that world and growled, "If I can't manipulate them with fear, I will have to open the book from the outside of the real world."

Meanwhile, back in Dark Woods on that dark and stormy night, three boys and one girl were walking through the forest looking for something and saying to themselves, "Oh, the world hates us, some people lose a pencil and a pen but we manage to lose a whole football."

The four were Jason and his best friends Shanna, Alex and Zach.

"This is why we should never play near the woods," Alex said. "Why do you have to kick the ball so hard, Jason? Now it could be anywhere, hidden under the shrubs and grass and trees."

"I must be stronger than I thought," Jason said. "I didn't know it would go so far into the woods when I kicked it. Did you see how far I threw that egg yesterday, Shanna?"

"Oh, here we go," Shanna groaned. "If we don't stop him, he'll start bragging about how strong he is."

"I'm not surprised I was the one to lose the ball," Jason said. "I keep losing things. My mum can't stand it. Remember that time I lost my bike, Shanna?"

"How on earth do you lose a bike? Were you riding it when you lost it?" Zach asked, and they laughed.

"Guys, it's getting dark. We need to find that ball before it's too dark to see anything," Shanna urged.

Just at that moment, Alex's foot hit a tree trunk. Something fell from the branch above. They saw that it had a pentagram symbol on it.

A Deadly Discovery

They hoped it would be some kind of treasure, but when they opened the door, they saw that it just had a device or a machine of some kind. When they pressed a button and pulled the trigger that was on it, nothing happened, and they turned to each other for a little talk about what a machine like this could possibly be doing in a tree.

"Strange, isn't it? Has a trigger but it's not a gun," Alex said.

"And these buttons. It doesn't look like an ordinary toy," Jason said, turning it around in his hand. It was rather light.

At that moment, Alex turned around as a mysterious journal appeared behind them. The little screen that had a pentagram symbol now flashed a number: 2.

Alex gasped and pointed. "Did you see that? It just appeared."

Shanna gasped. "Where did that come from?"

But as they were looking at the book, Jason spotted a letter on the right side of the journal's cover. It said: "My name is Journal #2, what's yours?"

They looked at the book with fear and curiosity, wondering where it had come from. When they opened it, it glowed purple and the words "property of…" appeared on the page. Without a name, they had no way of knowing whose journal it was.

They read the first entry. It read: "I can't believe that I have made more and more books this year. I hope I petrify everyone."

The book had so much information about monsters and the history of Dark Woods. The second entry read: "Unfortunately, I was wrong and my books can now bring my monsters to life and I'm now being watched, so I must hide these books before they find them; remember, trust no one!!!"

Not knowing what they were getting themselves into, they decided they had better solve the mystery of the journal and find the secret of its magic – not knowing that this was a mystery far beyond their imagination, and not knowing the danger they were in.

THE END

If you enjoyed The Scarecrow Lives at Night or any other books in the series, please leave a review so others can hear what you thought. Perhaps more importantly, I would love to hear if you liked the book, and what you liked? Thank you.

Made in United States
Orlando, FL
04 October 2025